D0800855

Greg's Second Adventure in Time

C. M. Huddleston
2015

Greg's Second Adventure in Time

Published by:
Interpreting Time's Past PRESS
Crab Orchard, Kentucky

Text and cover copyright © 2015 by C.M. Huddleston
All rights reserved. No part of this book may be used or reproduced in any manner whatsoever without written permission except in the case of brief quotations embodied in critical articles and reviews.
For information address Interpreting Time's Past, LLC, 450 Old Richmond Road, South, Crab Orchard, KY 40419

Cover by Interpreting Time's Past, LLC

ISBN: 978-0-9964304-2-5

Cover Image and p. 84: *Boonesborough Just Before the Siege* from Filson Club Publication 1901

p. iv "Daniel Boone" and p. 96 "Boone's Fight with Two Indians" from *Famous Frontiersmen, ~~Poineers~~ and Scouts* by E.G. Cattermole, 1884   Pioneers

p. 156 "Daniel Boone" from *The Life and Times of Col. Daniel Boone, Hunter Soldier and Pioneer* by Edward S. Ellis, 1884

For my parents,
Lena Carl "Sissa" Wade Aldridge
and Thomas Kenneth Aldridge
both proud Kentuckians

DANIEL BOONE.

Chapters

1
How It All Started

"Mom! Stop stabbing me with that pin," I whined.

"Greg, it's not a pin. It's a needle. Stand still and stop whimpering each time I accidentally stick you. You are not bleeding. Act like a 13-year-old instead of a child."

"But Mom, I am supposed to be Skyping with Rose," I pleaded. I mean, there I was standing in the living room being *fitted* for scratchy woolen trousers and a linen shirt. I needed to be online with Rose discussing my plans for the summer instead of being dressed in some ridiculous getup. I didn't even volunteer to be in the re-enactment at John Martin's Station. Mom volunteered me. She didn't even ask. Just assumed I would be willing.

Oh, hi! I'm Greg and I guess I'd better explain. Almost a whole year has passed since my first adventure in time travel. You know, when I traveled back 3,000 years and met Hopelf and all his family and visited his village? A lot happened during this last year. First, there was school. Then I wrote that scary, but true, "what I did last summer" essay telling about my time travel. That brought me nothing but grief. No one, and I do mean *no one* except Mom and Rose, believed me. I'm really not sure about Rose, but at least she pretended to believe me. Oh, you do remember Rose? She's the girl I met last year right after I time traveled back to the present. I do mean *right as I traveled back*. You'll just have to read about my first adventure in time travel if you want to know more.

Anyway, I was so miserable Mom pulled me out of school and planned to home school me for the rest of the year. Rose is home schooled too, by her father. He works from home—you know, he telecommutes. So our parents worked out a system, and we got to study together most days. I liked spending time with Rose and her father. They are a neat family. Rose's mom died a few years back. She doesn't talk about it much. I guess it still hurts. We spent a lot of time together.

I still talk a lot—actually, constantly when I am awake. I talk to myself, my computer, my books, Mom, Dad, Rose, and anyone willing to listen. I've always been like this—well . . . except when I time traveled last year and right off met an Indian boy with a spear. A spear pointed at me. But enough about that.

Back to this story, Dad came home just before Christmas, like always. Only this time, he had news. We were moving! To Kentucky! I'd never even been in Kentucky, didn't know what it was like, and really didn't want to know. But, Mom and I packed up the house. Dad had already reported to his new post. Mom found a new archaeological position, and we moved. I hated my new school—yes, I attended school again. I haven't made many friends. Dad was gone again, like always. I mean, if he was never going to be home, why did we have to move? I know, I know. I just need to get over it!

We live near Mom's work instead of near Fort Knox where Dad's stationed, so he really can't come home each night. It's just too far to drive. It still isn't fair. Mom says life isn't fair. It should be!

Mom's archaeological excavations were at a place called John Martin's Station, one of the first settlements in Kentucky—back before the Revolutionary War. You know, way back in the 1770s. Mom led the dig and worked there most days instead of being at her laboratory in town. So we lived in Paris—Kentucky, not France— where I went to school and where Mom's lab was located. Paris was okay, I guess. Not great. It was a bit larger than the town where we lived in Maryland.

Finally, the school year came to an end in late May, because we had no snow days. Strange to live in a place with very little snow. Mom planned for me to work with her again during the summer break. You know the drill, I'd excavate and "teach" the kids that come to archaeology camp. I guess it's not *awful*, but I

4

had hoped to see Rose and maybe take a vacation to somewhere *cool*. As in *neat* cool, not weather cool. But, you see, archaeologists take advantage of warm weather for most of their excavation time. They do their lab work in the winter and on rainy days. So, no vacation. It wouldn't be any fun without Dad, anyway.

So here I was, hiding in my room, getting ready to Skype with Rose. Mom continued shouting occasionally at me to come back and read the history she'd set aside. She wanted me to read up on John Martin's Station and a book on Daniel Boone. Little did she know I had already read it—well, most of it. I read the part on Martin's Station, I skipped the list of names of people who lived near there. Boring! I had started the book on Boone.

Okay! Finally, Rose rang in on Skype. You know the voice-over-internet provider. I love Skype because this way we could see each other while talking—so much better than on the phone.

"Hi, how was your day?" she asked quietly.

"Okay. School is finally out, but Mom is

making me a re-enactment costume and keeps sticking me with the needle. She is sewing the pants, shirt, and jacket strictly by hand—no sewing machine. Can you imagine all that time and work? It's taking her fore-v-e-r. Besides, I have to keep trying it on—you know a *fitting*. Then she bought me these leather shoes. Did you know that in the 18th century they didn't have left and right shoes? I mean, they feel weird. Stiff, not at all like my sneakers. Can you believe the pants are wool, and they itch and have this weird button panel in the front instead of a zipper? The shirt is linen. It itches too. She is even making a jacket. It's summer and hot, why do I need a jacket? I don't . ."

"Greg, you are rambling. Stop talking," she demanded slowly emphasizing each word.

So I shut up and looked at her closely and realized something terrible had happened. Her dark amber eyes shone with tears, and she looked like she has been crying for hours. "Rose, what's wrong?" I asked.

"Dad says I have to spend this summer with my aunt and uncle in Idaho! Greg, they live on a sheep farm and don't even have internet!

Can you believe they don't own a computer? They live 45 miles from a town, if you can call it a town. It has only 651 residents! No library, no theater, nothing, really!"

"Now who was babbling!" I thought, but before I could interrupt she started in again. Girls!

"They have eleven children! Eleven! Who has eleven children? I can't imagine why they want me to visit. I mean Dad is going to Africa on business, but I could stay with someone else."

"Who?" I asked. "Just who would you stay with?" Then my brain clicked and I said, "Wait, you could stay with us instead! Let me go ask Mom. I'll call back. No, don't go anywhere! Stay right there. It'll just take a minute." And I was off, running down the stairs, bouncing off walls and yelling "Mom" the whole way.

Like usual I had to stop and listen to Mom fuss about my *unruly behavior*. While fidgeting, I bounced from one foot to another, waiting for her to wind down. Finally, she paused for a breath, and I poured out Rose's whole sad story about Idaho.

"Yes, I know," Mom replied, quite matter of factly.

"You know?"

"Yes, Greg, I know. Her father and I spoke last week when he realized he had to go to Entebbe. That's in Uganda, in case you didn't know. We decided it would be better if Rose visited her mother's sister, than stay here. I offered to let her stay, but he decided on Idaho," Mom explained. She sounded concerned.

"Mom, is everything okay?" I asked tentatively.

"Oh, I'm just a bit worried about Matthew (Rose's dad). Africa isn't a safe place to work right now," she replied with even more concern.

"Just exactly what does her Dad do?" I asked.

"Military logistical supply," she explained, "making sure our special forces soldiers have everything they need. It's a very important job."

So, I went back up, explained to Rose what Mom had said, and listened to her complain.

So, that's how my summer started. Bummer. Right?

2
Time Travel

So, nothing else to do, I decided to research time travel theories. I mean I have done it—twice—time travel that is, not research it. Once back 3,000 years and then forward to my own time. But I have no idea how. I had been meaning to do this bit of research for a while but, well, I just didn't get around to it. So, I Googled time travel.

Did you know there are three main theories of time travel? The first says that time is a *fixed line*. No matter what you do when you travel back in time you cannot change the future. It seems the actions you take in the past have already happened because you were already there doing them. It's just like in *Harry Potter and the Prisoner of Azkaban* where Hermione and Harry go back to free Sirius Black. So when I went back and saved Hopelf, I didn't change history because it had already happened. Really confusing.

Then there is one alternate theory that says if you go back in time you can alter history because we live in a *dynamic timeline*. This theory was used in some old movie Mom and Dad like to watch called *Back to the Future*. The hero of that story was Marty McFly! Really, McFly? I'd change my name if it was McFly!

If that theory were true then when I went back in time and saved Hopelf after the bear attacked him, I changed history. But how are we to know? I mean it was prehistory—before written language. No one would ever know if I saved one Native American from an agonizing death. But then again, if I had died while in that time, it would have changed my history. If I died while back there 3,000 years ago, could I have been born? Or, was I born and then died all over again? How many times have I been born and died? This theory is even more confusing than first one.

Finally, I discovered a third theory of time travel. It's the scariest of all. It calls for all these *parallel universes* traveling toward the future. So if you go back and change the past, it becomes a new timeline. But if you are not careful then you may change history so that you never exist. I think I exist? I did time travel. Did I change time? If this is a parallel universe, are there more than one of me? Oh, this is so confusing.

Maybe, I should just figure out *how* I time traveled. I didn't use a time machine or a Delorian, that's a car, like in *Back to the Future*. I didn't touch mystical stones like in some book Mom read called *Outlander* where the lady put her hands on standing stones like at Stonehenge. That would be cool since Stonehenge is a fantastic archaeological site, but there were no ancient standing stones in Creasaptown, Maryland. I mean, all I did was pick up a projectile point and . . . stand there? Was it that easy? Mom kept telling me to make sure I didn't lose her trowel in my dreams while I was time traveling. Yet, when I got home she just laughed about it being *magical* and said she just really likes that particular trowel.

I didn't feel weird when it happened. No rushing through time. No popping noises. I was just here and then just there.

So no time machine, no magical trowel, and Mom can time travel too?

"How many people can time travel?" I asked Mom once.

Her answer was brief, "Only a few." Then she changed the subject. What kind of mom is she? Won't even answer life's most very important questions!

So, I called Dad and asked him, but he laughed—then changed the subject. What aren't they telling me?

Can I just pick a place and time and go there? Can I become a French Musketeer? I would love to learn how to sword fight, save the king, and things. Looks like fun! Guess I'd have to learn French. Could I see the real Battle of

Gettysburg? We went to a Civil War battlefield for a re-enactment before we moved last year. It was cool!

I would like to visit Hopelf. But how?

Feeling a bit confused, I remembered there are several avenues of research. Hey, I live with a scientist. You have to answer the questions who, what, when, where, why, and how. Just like a journalist writing a newspaper article or preparing a story for the evening news. Or maybe these six questions only refer to journalism. *Whatever!* I thought it would work if I tried to find the answers to these six questions.

I knew who, Mom and I and a few others, according to her, can time travel. What is time travel? Well, that's obvious! When can people time travel? No idea. Where? Again, no idea. Why? Because it's *cool* was my first answer. But is that *really* the reason a few people can time travel? I doubted it.

Then there was HOW? The question that started this whole thing. I thought about it for a while, maybe a minute before being distracted.

So, I picked up the Boone book, read for a bit, and went to sleep.

3
Archaeology & Stations

So time passed. Rose remained in *nowhere* Idaho. Dad couldn't even call from wherever he was. May turned hot and humid, and I was once more excavating with Mom. Historic digs, it turns out are mostly just like prehistoric ones, except you find different types of artifacts and can use written history to learn about the site and who lived there.

Instead of projectile points and bits of broken clay pots, we found nails, window glass, bottle glass, European-made ceramics (bits of dishes), pewter, clay pipe fragments, etc. Did you know that during Colonial times the men smoked these long, really long-stemmed white clay pipes? Weird!

We also found buttons, glass shirt buttons and large pewter coat buttons. These came off men's clothing. Most women's clothing didn't have buttons. Their dresses laced up or were pinned—with straight pins! Zippers and even safety pins hadn't been invented yet.

We found Indian stuff too. It seems the frontier folk liked to collect projectile points and other artifacts just like some people do now. Of course, sometimes a frontier family would build their cabin right on top of a prehistoric site. I guess they both appreciated a good piece of land. Anyway, that's where we worked every day, shoveling off the top layer of soil, you know the plowzone, and looking for features.

Some local people volunteered each day at the dig to screen the soil for artifacts and help in any way they could. The local archaeological society brought at least seven people each day. They took turns digging, screening, and even washing artifacts under a big tent they erected.

The tent's sides rolled up and allowed for lots of natural light and sometimes a breeze. I liked to hide out there at lunch. They kept cold soft drinks in a big cooler.

The volunteers washed the artifacts in small basins with water from a nearby spring. Mom found it in a limestone outcropping her first day on the site. The spring sat in a small valley and drained back underground a few feet away. It developed over thousands of years as the movement of water underground ate away the bedrock and bubbled to the surface. The local residents say it never goes dry, even in the hot months of late summer. Some say that after particularly heavy rains, the water often shoots up several feet into the air like a geyser. That's called an artesian head. *Cool.* I wish I could see it shoot off.

Pioneer folk needed water near their homes. So they built near streams, rivers, and springs. Spring water in Kentucky is usually clear and clean, because it's filtered through the area's limestone bedrock. While 200 years ago it was safe to drink, it isn't now! The water is filtered through the bedrock, and all that time spent underground allows debris and mud to fall to the bottom. But, microbes, viruses, and bacteria do not die just from being underground. Also, industrial and farming pollutants remain in the water. But it sure looked clean. Mom just about throttled me when I attempted to drink from the spring our first day on the site.

So, I spent the first days of my summer, excavating at what Mom hoped was the site of John Martin's Station. The frontiersmen built stations which were small forts or fortified dwellings where people could take shelter during Indian raids. Central Kentucky was once dotted with small stations surrounded by small farms.

When the first settlers came across the Appalachian Mountains and through Cumberland Gap from Virginia or floated down the Ohio River from Fort Pitt (now Pittsburgh) into *Kentuck*, no Indians lived in the central portion of the region.

This central portion is now called the *Bluegrass* and is surrounded by a series of low hills called the *Knobs*. Back then the area had rolling grasslands and heavy forests along the banks of the Kentucky, Elkhorn, and Licking rivers. It must have looked pretty inviting to those pioneers.

Indians from surrounding areas used the region's eastern and southern mountains, the Bluegrass region, and the Cumberland and Ohio river valleys for hunting and trapping. The Cherokee, who lived to the southeast, and the Shawnee, Iroquois, and Wyandots, who lived to the north, along with several other tribes, claimed these hunting grounds. Sometimes they warred amongst themselves, but mostly they shared the land. They hunted bison, deer, elk, and bear. They caught fish, beaver, and otter in the rivers and streams.

So, the Indians considered the whole of *Kentuck* to be their garden. In these *happy hunting grounds*, they could not only hunt and fish but could gather nuts and berries. They found wild grapes, pawpaws, persimmons, wild cherries, and bee trees full of honey. If the winter was cold enough, the sugar maples produced a watery syrup that could be collected and boiled down to make maple syrup.

So just imagine how they felt when the settlers came into their hunting grounds and killed their wild animals, ate their nuts and berries, and stayed! These intruders built log homes by cutting down the trees. They cut down forests and pulled up the stumps and planted crops. Their livestock, like cattle, pigs, sheep, horses, and even fowl (chickens, geese, and ducks), ate the resources the Indians believed belonged to them. They became even more angry when these people claimed to own the land.

Other white men, like the British and French, also believed they owned this land. The French and British hated each other and fought over the land. They both wanted to control the land west of the Appalachian Mountains where *Kentuck* was located. So they riled up the Indians against each other's settlers by paying money for white scalps or for white prisoners. So you can see why these settlers needed forts and stations.

Do you know what scalping is? I wasn't absolutely sure so I looked it up. It means cutting or tearing a part, or all, of the human scalp, with its hair attached, off the head. The scalp was like a trophy and often worn on an Indian's belt! They did this to *live* people as well as dead people. First they would grab the person's hair and then make several semicircular cuts on either side of the head. Then they just yanked real hard. I think it must have really hurt. Most people who were scalped died from their wounds, but a few survived. Of course, they didn't have any hair and had to have their scalp sewn back together.

Indians were not the only group that scalped people. In our country's early history, the English scalped Indians and the French. The French scalped the English. And bad people scalped anyone just to get paid for a scalp. Really! Pretty, gross! Can you imagine not having skin on the top of your head. What would hold your face up?

Anyhow, back to the excavations. Other archaeologists and some historians have searched for Martin's Station but never found it. Several old letters and deeds told where the station once stood. Mom learned that while doing historic research at libraries and archives before she began the project. Martin's Station was even drawn on a plat or map used in some old lawsuit about who owned the land. The plat clearly shows the station near a large bend in Stoner Creek.

All those earlier archaeologists looked carefully all over the area, but no remains of the fortified station or even any historic artifacts could be found. Mom started looking again because the Commonwealth of Kentucky hired Mom to look near another bend in the creek where historic artifacts were recently uncovered by a local farmer.

The local historical and archaeological societies planned a re-enactment and "dig" for Saturday, June 13th. Mom expected me to show up in that silly costume and give tours of the archaeological site. I had planned to go, as there was nothing much else to do. Rose planned to be at a rodeo! I would love to go to a rodeo, but I live in Kentucky, not Idaho. I hoped she would have fun. She seemed so down each time I talked to her.

4
Saturday, 13 June 2015

I remember waking up to Mom's cell phone ringing somewhere in the house and wondering if it was Dad. I hadn't talked to him in weeks. He had to call soon, right? Mom didn't seem the least bit worried he hadn't called. I turned over to catch a few more minutes of sleep.

Before I could dose off again, Mom knocked on my door and told me to wake up and get dressed as we had to make a stop before we went to the dig site. Some kind of "archaeology emergency." That usually means someone has uncovered a skeleton. Part of Mom's job included checking out such finds. People report them to local sheriffs or police. They call the Office of State Archaeology at the University of Kentucky, and they send an archaeologist to check it out.

I could tell the day was going to be a hot one, and here I was dressing in wool trousers! Mom had purchased an authentic leather knapsack, which I filled with my pocket knife, compass, sneakers, the Daniel Boone book, and a few Cookies & Creme candy bars, my favorite. I always plan ahead where food is concerned. I put some other things in my pockets, just in case I might need them. Besides, I always carry my cell phone.

At the last minute I tied the sleeves of the costume's jacket around the straps of the knapsack. I doubted I would need a jacket but Mom worked so hard on it. I didn't want to hurt her feelings. Also, the volunteers planned a barbeque for the end of the re-enactment. Sometimes it turned cool in the evening.

Mom and I drove to a place about three miles north east of the Martin's Station excavations. Sure enough, I was right. There stood a sheriff's car, a farm truck which held an irate Australian Shepherd dog, and a couple of large tractors. The sheriff, several men, and a boy, a little older than I, stood in a group near a grove of trees along a rock-bottomed creek filled with slowly running water. Mom and I walked toward the men as they approached. We listened to their story about how the skeleton had been uncovered.

Using a cultivator pulled by a tractor, they had been working to turn over the rich soil near the banks of the Hinkston's Fork. They planned a late corn crop for this bit of bottom land. The farmer's son had been driving the tractor and had glanced along the creek as he was driving. I think driving a tractor around in circles must be pretty boring. That's when he saw the dog pulling the jaw bone out of the creek bank.

I stopped as we neared the truck to pet the dog, actually a half-grown pup. She was a beauty, a red-tricolor named Katy according to the tag on her collar. She vigorously wagged her backside—Aussies don't have tails—as I approached the truck. The boy yelled up that she was friendly, but not to let her out. It seemed she had run all over the field with her *treasure* before they had managed to catch her and take it away. She was still panting heavily, drooling all over the seats and my hand. She had a bowl of water with her on the truck's seat, but didn't seem interested in drinking. I guess she wanted to explore for more bones. I didn't dare open the truck door since she would have tried to escape, so I petted her through a half-open window.

After a short while, Mom yelled for me to bring her equipment pack. It always contains her favorite trowels, a camera, measuring tapes, levels, maps, note pads and pencils, Sharpies, bug spray, and artifact bags. Figuring we would be here awhile and not having had much breakfast, I grabbed my knapsack as well and slung it over my shoulder. I guess I looked kind of funny dressed as I was, because the sheriff, the men, and the boy all stared. So, I swept my arm out to the side and bowed from the waist. My hat fell off. Darn.

Mom proceeded to shoo them all away from the discovery and carefully went to work. Mom is not trained as a physical anthropologist, but she can recognize an old skeleton and tell it from a more recent burial. This one had an arrowhead buried in the right shoulder and one in the breastbone—a dead give away (pun intended) it was an ancient burial. Not many people are shot with Indian arrows nowadays!

Mom photographed the entire site before drawing a sketch map and marking the site on a quadrangle map that showed we were on Hinkston's Fork of the South Fork of the Licking River. She took a GPS reading with her phone and marked the info on the map as well. Next, she would call the State Archaeologist's office and report the find so it could be examined more thoroughly. Maybe she would excavate here next. Who knows?

Meanwhile, I took some pictures to send to Rose and Dad with my camera phone, waded barefoot in the creek, ate a candy bar, and tried to skip rocks. The water wasn't very deep. Basically, I was bored. I had just picked up my shoes and finished lacing them back on when I noticed what I thought was a deer hide sticking out of the bank near the skeleton. I walked over to point it out to Mom. She continued to be distracted by her maps and the skeleton and paid me no mind. So I reached down to brush off some of the dirt and rotted leaves. I bent lower to examine my find and had just touched the hide when it happened.

I time traveled - AGAIN!

5
Saturday, 13 June 1778

There I stood surrounded by Indians! **Again!** Okay, there was only one Indian last time, and he was just a boy. This time there were five! Five! I counted them twice! There sat five of them! Grown men! With tomahawks and war paint! On the bank just above where the skeleton had been. I know because now it was a dead body with two arrows sticking out of it. It had no hair, just a bloody skull.

They, the Indians, all five of them, seemed focused on a turkey roasting over a small fire.

It smelled delicious. But when a boy pops into your world from nowhere, you react. And they did.

All five scrambled to their feet, picked up their weapons, and advanced toward me. Not real fast, but I didn't care. I couldn't seem to run, just stood there. One Indian seemed older than the rest. He held up his hand signaling them to stop. So, I tried a peaceful greeting in Hopelf's language—he was an Indian so I thought it might work! It didn't—might as well have been speaking Greek.

Next I tried English. That seemed to work. Well, at least with one of them. He looked at me suspiciously and then replied.

"How you get here? Where from you come?"

"Oh, no, here we go with the questions again." I thought.

But this time I was more prepared and less afraid. Instead of answering, I dropped my knapsack off my shoulder, bowed—my hat fell off again—and reached into my pocket at the same time. I pulled out a soft ball, about the size of a ping pong ball, and what looked like a regular golf ball.

That's when I began singing loudly, "I'd like to teach the world to sing in perfect harmony, I'd like to see the world for once all standing hand in hand, and hear them echo through the hills, for peace throughout the land, I'd like to teach the world to sing in perfect harmony . . ."

I kept singing that part over and over again because those were the only words I remembered! The song came from some old Coke-a-Cola commercial Mom likes. She sings it while washing dishes, cooking, and even in the shower. She knows all the words.

I kind of hate to admit this, but I also danced a little jig sort of dance, kind of a mixture between soft shoe and clogging. But the really spectacular part came when I threw the exploding golf ball against a rock creating a loud bang and a large cloud of dust. It just so happened the Indians had plucked the turkey in that exact spot and with the cloud of dust billowed a cloud of turkey feathers. Two of the

Indians began sneezing violently. Those little, white down feathers flew everywhere. It was really something to see and hear. I would have laughed, but I was still too scared.

Then I squeezed the smaller ball hard and created a flash of light in my hands. The trick only works once or twice, but the second time was enough. All five Indians grabbed their belongings and disappeared into the surrounding forest. They all stared at me as they left, but I just kept singing and dancing as I reached for another exploding magic trick. Good thing they departed, as I only had one more of each trick left in my pockets.

Mom once told me that American Indians, like most primitive cultures, were often wary of things they did not understand. I guess that's why the flashes of light in my hands and the exploding golf ball made them leave. I don't think they were afraid, just wary of my magic.

Of course, it could have been my singing and dancing. I'm not very good at either. Mom says I have a tin ear and two left feet. In those shoes, I looked like I do.

So there I stood, somewhere back in history. No idea when, but I had an idea, at least about what year it was. I had time traveled when I touched the deer hide. There it lay, right next to the dead guy.

I walked over carefully, while keeping a wary eye out for the Indians, just in case they decided to come back. He, the dead body, was definitely dead, and he had been scalped. He also had several knife wounds as well as the two arrows sticking out of him.

He was dressed in buckskin trousers, a cotton shirt, a deerskin jacket, and leather moccasins. He had a sheath for a knife and a powder horn, but I couldn't find his rifle or his knife. He looked to be about 30 years of age, once had red hair, and lots of freckles. A pack lay nearby, so I examined its contents. I found rifle balls and wadding, a wrapper containing salt, some corn pone, a clean shirt, dried venison, and a blanket rolled along the top. I used the blanket to cover the body.

Finally, I picked up the deer hide. Someone had neatly wrapped part of a hide around an oilcloth bundle. The hide protected the oilcloth which kept the contents dry. I carefully cut the twine (with my knife) that tied it shut and discovered a bunch of letters. Each letter had a name and one of Kentucky's stations or forts written on the outside. Most didn't have envelopes, but were just the letter itself folded into a neat square.

I don't think the dead man was a mail man, probably just someone who had been traveling to the frontier and had been asked to carry the letters. Travelers would carry letters from people back east to the various stations and leave them to be picked up.

I felt bad about his death, but even more so about my situation. I didn't know what year it was but from the date on one of the letters, I guessed it might be 1778, probably the 13th of June. If I was correct, then the Revolutionary War continued in the eastern colonies, and Kentucky was under almost constant attack from roving Indians.

I decided the better part of valor might be to move away from the area and try to find Martin's Station. I picked up my knapsack and the dead man's pack. I wrapped the letters back in the oilcloth and stuffed them in the pack. But I left the deer hide right where I had dropped it.

So I had just created Mom's archaeological find. I left the body with nothing but its clothing and the arrows sticking out of it. By the time Mom examined the remains, the river cane arrow shafts and his clothing had rotted away. So Mom only found the skeleton with the two arrow heads. I had found the deer hide.

After a moment, I pulled out my compass and started walking.

6
Not Lost,
Just Bewildered

I learned to read a compass a couple of years ago at a wilderness camp. It's a good skill to know, and I'm actually very good. Based on where Mom found the skeleton and where I thought the Martin's Station dig was located, I set my direction and started out. I also thought the creek might be either Stoner or a tributary of the Licking River. I should have taken a better look at Mom's map. But I had never expected to time travel and need that particular information.

Now, Daniel Boone once said he was never lost, just *bewildered* for days at a time. I kind of felt the same way. Walking along the creek, I noticed somewhat of a path, like animals and men had walked beside the creek many times. I walked for about a half hour before I heard voices. They were not speaking English. I could not understand a word they said. So I hid down low behind some dense undergrowth and waited. After only a few minutes, I could no longer hear them talking. I crept out of my hiding spot and continued moving silently along the path.

I kept thinking that maybe following the path might not be such a good idea. Obviously, Indians used it. But it followed the creek and seemed to be taking me in the general direction of where I thought Martin's Station might be. On the other hand, I knew if my mind wandered, or if I did not listen carefully, I might just walk into more Indians. I might not be able to sing and dance my way out of trouble the next time.

The day grew hotter and hotter. I rolled up my shirt sleeves and pants' legs to get more air. Wool and linen are not really cool fabrics. Once or twice, I splashed water from the creek on my face and head to cool off. I had to resort to drinking from the creek as I had nothing with me to drink. I figured if it didn't kill the pioneers it wouldn't kill me.

I don't know how long I walked since I'd left my wristwatch at home that morning. Remember, I was wearing this stupid costume, and wristwatches had not yet been invented. I guess, given the circumstances, that turned out to be a good thing. At least if I met up with pioneer Kentuckians, which I sincerely hoped I would, I knew I would look like I belonged in their time.

I spent my time while walking thinking up a believable story about how a boy happened to be all alone in the wilderness of *Kentuck*. I came up with what I thought was a good tale. Short, sweet, and easy to remember.

Several hours passed before I heard other human voices. They seemed to be speaking a mixture of German and English. I had lived in Germany as a child and still remembered a few words of German. I crept forward toward the sounds and looked through a break in the trees. A man and a boy worked to tie a rope around a small tree stump. A mule tied to the other end of the rope grazed peacefully awaiting their commands. I listened for a minute or two before deciding it was safe to make myself known to them.

I called out first, "Hey, the camp!"

Both the boy and the man jumped. The man dropped the rope and picked up a nearby Kentucky long rifle I had not even noticed. The boy picked up a musket just as the man yelled out, "Who approaches?"

"My name is Greg, and I'm alone," I yelled as I stepped from the cover of the trees into the newly cleared area. I could tell most of the trees had recently been cut and figured they were clearing the land to plant crops.

Both of them stared, but lowered their weapons and just stood there watching the tree line behind me. I walked to where they were working and stuck out my hand.

"My name is Greg. I was traveling with a party to Boonesborough when we were attacked by Indians. I ran, and then couldn't find my companions. I've been traveling alone

42

for a couple of days. I found a man's body this morning. Killed by Indians. Where am I? Can you help me?" I said all of this in my usual *don't know when to stop talking way*, kind of out of breath, trying to make them believe I really was scared and relieved to find help. Actually, I was. Relieved to find help, that is.

Edmund Rittenhouse introduced himself and his son, Samuel. He offered me water, a bit of cornbread, and some venison jerky to eat. We sat on some stumps still standing in the field, and I told my story. My made-up story, that is. I told of coming through the Gap with our party of seven men including my father and brother. I told of how we got lost going to Boonesborough, the Indian attack, my escape, the dead man, and my trip along the creek. I don't know why I made up a brother, but it seemed to add realism to my story.

Mr. Rittenhouse told me I had followed Hinkston's Fork. This fork joined Stoner Creek near Martin's Station. His son sat quietly and listened.

At last, I handed him the dead man's pack with the letters and showed him what I had learned. He thought he knew who the young man might be when I mentioned his red hair and freckles. He knew he was right when he opened the packet of letters and saw one addressed to his wife Sarah from her friend back in Pennsylvania and several more for folks at Martin's Station.

That's when he offered me the frontier hospitality of his home and food until we figured out how to get me to Boonesborough to meet up with my imaginary father and brother. I had actually planned to go back to where I had time traveled, but didn't say as much. I thought I would need to go there to return to my time. At least that's how I got home the last time I time traveled.

We gathered up all the tools, unhitched the mule, and started along a short, barely visible path to their cabin. The sun began to set as we walked quietly. I learned from Edmund they suspected Indian activity in the area and always walked in silence. Tired, I kept my thoughts to myself and hoped I was doing the right thing. I had not planned on an adventure that morning. Yet, here I was again, far from home, not in distance, but in time.

7
A Frontier Cabin

Neither man nor boy called out as we approached the cabin. The clearing around the single pen cabin contained a rough fenced lot which held a horse. A strange looking wagon stood nearby. I thought it might have been created from pieces as it looked somewhat curious except for its wheels. A few chickens scratched in a yard covered overhead with woven vines and leaves, built to protect them from hawks and eagles. Behind the cabin I could see a rough lean-to with a wash kettle and stacks of fire wood.

The single-pen, squared-log cabin, measured about 16 feet by 16 feet had a rough single roof. What Mom always called a *cats and clay* chimney arose on one end. It looked like a bunch of small logs embedded in mortar that reached as high as the ridge pole of the cabin. I knew this type chimney was easier to build than a stone chimney. Pioneers often put them on new cabins until enough stones had been found while the fields were being cleared to erect a chimney from stone. The cabin had one window on the front. There was no glass, but shutters flanked each side. Someone had built a door of rough puncheon, logs finished flat on one side only. It stood open, hanging from wood and leather hinges and had a string latch.

The rich smell of roasting meat wafted from the cabin and a slight curl of pale gray smoke arose from the chimney. A small, blonde girl, about two years of age, rushed out the front door and yelled, "Samuel, Samuel, Samuel," over and over again. He picked her up and carried her the rest of the way to back to the cabin.

Another girl, who I thought might be about ten years old, walked into the clearing from the direction of the creek carrying two heavy buckets of water. I placed my belongings on a nearby stump and rushed over to help her.

Keeping her head lowered, she stammered "Danke" (thank-you in German) as I took both buckets from her hands.

Not knowing how many members of the Rittenhouse family lived in the small cabin, I waited for more to pour out. But it seemed I had met them all except Mrs. Rittenhouse. Edmund's wife Sarah stepped to the door about that time, and we were introduced. The youngest girl's name was Leah, and the oldest was Abigail.

Frontier hospitality required I be given food and shelter. I knew I was expected to pitch in and help with the chores. Samuel and I carried in firewood, split more for the next day, fed the pigs and chickens, and hobbled the mule. I had never hobbled an animal before. It proved to be rather difficult as the mule was very stubborn. Samuel and I had to buckle heavy leather bands connected by a leather strap around his front legs just above the hoof. This way he could move about, but not walk fast or wander far off.

As dusk arrived, Sarah called us all in for the evening meal. After a reading from their German Bible, which I didn't understand, Edmund gave a short prayer, and we ate. A rich stew of rabbit with bits of root vegetables served as the main course. Some early summer greens and a pan of thick cornbread with fresh butter helped fill our stomachs. While Leah drank milk, the rest of us shared dippers of cold water.

The cabin's interior held a rough table with two benches, a nice cherry rocker, a carved oak cradle, and a platform bed built into the wall. The brightly colored bed linens added to the hominess of the small dark cabin. Against the wall stood a crude ladder used to reach a small loft above the bed. Samuel told me this was where he slept and helped me put my belongings in the loft.

Above the massive fire hearth, a shelf held carved wooden bowls, some pewter spoons, a few knives, and two books. I checked them out and discovered both were in German. Next to the hearth stood two additional cooking pots. One of these had three legs, Mom called these *spiders*. A butter churn and a jug stood in the corner behind the table. Above the bed, a row of pegs on the wall held some clothing, extra shirts, a skirt, some shawls, and a crocheted sweater for Leah.

When we entered the cabin, Edmund and Samuel hung their firearms on pegs near the door. Each also hung up their powder horn, and shot pouch. I noticed crude hemp ropes allowed the shutters to be closed from the inside. The back of the cabin had a window as well. Two rifle slits were cut into the logs near the front door and two near the back window. Two more flanked the chimney, as did two on the opposite wall.

After the meal, Abigail washed the bowls and helped her mother clear away the cooking things. Samuel and I carried in more water from the creek. We made sure the animals had water and finished up the chores just after dark.

Samuel wasn't very talkative. This gave me time to assess my situation. I figured with all the Indian activity in the area I had better stay put for a few days. I had been surprised to find a small, printed calendar on the cabin wall and saw the year 1778. The day was 13 June. If I had tried, I could not have traveled to colonial *Kentuck* at a worse time!

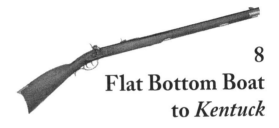

8
Flat Bottom Boat
to *Kentuck*

Edmund closed the cabin door and swung the heavy wood latch in place. Sarah lit hickory bark pieces instead of candles to give us a bit of light, as Edmund picked up his pipe and filled it with tobacco. I didn't know what the evening would bring, until Edmund asked me to tell Sarah my harrowing story of escape from the Indians. He had previously handed over her letter and told of the courier's death.

Quietly and without exaggeration I told my tale. I left out the part about the song and the exploding golf ball. I did tell about the ball that would make a flash of light in my hands. Samuel expressed his curiosity about where I came about such a trick.

After giving him a vague answer about things that could be purchased in the colonies, I asked Edmund how long they had been in *Kentuck*. Now came the time for him to tell their story.

Throughout the meal and the earlier part of the day, Edmund had been quiet and seemed even a bit shy. Now as he began telling their story, his eyes shone bright blue and his voice and laughter filled the cabin.

"Oh, my, we came almost two years ago— two years ago it will be in September, just Sarah, Samuel, Abigail, and I down the Ohio River in a flat boat. What an adventure that was! Never been so frightened in my life. But I must begin our story before that time.

"You see until 1775, Sarah and I lived in Pennsylvania with her parents. Oh, no, no, I must start much further back, back at my beginning. You see, I came to America in 1765, not much more than a boy myself, from Trier, Germany. I was the youngest of seven children, all boys, nary a girl amongst us. So, my parents sent me to live with my uncle in America to learn to be a tailor. I didn't want to be a tailor, but traveling to America seemed a good adventure, even if it did mean becoming an indentured servant to pay my crossing. Little did I know where that journey would take me!

"You see, when I arrived In Pennsylvania, I discovered my uncle had died not long before. As his family could not afford to pay my passage, the ship's captain put me on the block to find a master willing to pay for my crossing. It just so happened, a German, like myself, stood in the crowd looking for a new apprentice. When the captain announced I could only speak German, he offered to pay my fees if I would agree to seven years labor. So, that day I became an indentured servant to Sarah's father, a wheelwright.

"I think that day started my life. I liked being a wheelwright better than being a tailor. Besides, I met my Sarah. As you can see, young Greg, my Sarah is fair of face, intelligent, a willing worker, and a good mother. How could I not fall in love at first sight with such a girl? She even taught me the English her family spoke at home.

"Now, my indenture lasted only five years, instead of seven. During that time, Sarah and I fell in love and married. Her father revoked my last two years as a wedding gift. Our Samuel arrived later that same year and Abigail three years later.

"When Sarah's father released me from my service, we continued to live and work together as one big family. Then in 1775, I joined the colonists for a while and marched on Boston. That's a story for another day when just us men have time to spare. I wanted to fight for my new country. When, my term ended, I returned home to find that Sarah labored alone as both her parents had contracted a fever and died during my absence. Our farm and workshop were lost.

"You see, many of our more wealthy neighbors held with the Crown. So, my service with the patriots made us the enemy. Now, these were men and women we had known for years;

yet, they took our land and home and workshop. Sarah and our babes had lived with patriot friends during the last part of my absence.

"What was I to do? I believe the future of America cannot include a ruler with an iron hand, making taxes from across a wide ocean. We have partitioned for independence. I have read Mr. Jefferson's Declaration and agree with his ideas. I am a patriot like most men in *Kentuck*.

"With little left to us, Sarah and I packed up just one wagon with this rocking chair and cradle that once belonged to her mother, our few personal belongings, and our children and headed west to Fort Pitt. We traveled with others for safety and arrived in early summer. Along the way, little Edmund, our third child, died of scarlet fever. Samuel and Abigail suffered as well, but thanks to God's blessings, they survived.

"All along Sarah and I had planned to buy land near Fort Pitt where I believed my craft would provide us with a sufficient income. Being as it sits at the confluence of the Allegheny and Monongahela rivers, right where the Ohio River begins, I thought all those wagons coming inland bringing supplies and those going further west would oft need repairing. A boat building enterprise near the fort employed many men. That gave me hope of success for this business venture.

"But Fort Pitt, a cesspool of all kinds of humanity, left much to be desired as a new home. Wagons, hundreds of wagons, came and went monthly. I kept busy and made money doing repairs, for the western roads are mostly barely-cleared paths cut through dense forests with stumps and stones making the way rough and dangerous.

"The wagoners, lumbermen, and soldiers at the fort constantly drank and swore loudly. The encampment of tents offered no security or warmth for my family. Most of the families, like ours, had little left among them. They shared food and provisions and watched out for each other. But fevers and other ailments made the camp unhealthy.

"In 1776, while repairing a rudder for a Colonel John Hinkston's flatboat, I received an offer. The good Colonel needed families for his settlement in *Kentuck*. Men with skills were much in demand. I had money saved to buy land,

and the Colonel had an extra flatboat headed down the Ohio on which my family could travel. Sarah and I discussed the opportunity and, despite the Indian trouble, we decided to go. We figured the new stations at Hinkston's and Martin's would provide shelter in times of trouble.

"So, although it be late in the season, we packed our belongings, bought supplies to carry us through the winter, and joined the party going west to *Kentuck*. Two other families and several menfolk traveled with us. The Colonel had six boats all roped together and loaded with supplies for his settlements.

"Our flat boat measured only about seven feet wide and twelve feet long. Rough wood sides stood all around, about five feet high. These helped protect us from bullets and arrows and kept children and livestock from falling overboard. Built of green oak planks held together by wooden pins, the boat builder had sealed the seams with pitch and tow. With its flat hull, we knew we could float down rivers where more traditional boats would flounder. It was late in the season, and many of the streams, once we left the Ohio, would be shallow. A small shelter built atop, provided some protection from the elements for my family, while our livestock stood tethered at the rear.

"The first few days proved uneventful as we drifted downstream, staying always in the middle of the river. One man on each boat kept a look out with a loaded weapon ready to protect us from Indians or river pirates. The days grew hotter and hotter, but we kept the boats tied together and never approached the shore if we could help it. We ate cold food, drank river water, and watched the shores for signs of danger. We knew the 600 miles to our new home would take weeks of travel.

"As we drifted along the river in Virginia, we stopped at a small settlement called Marietta to purchase additional shot and powder. That proved to be our last sight of honest white men until we reached *Kentuck*, for only two nights later, river pirates in canoes tried to overtake our party. One man in the last flatboat died of his wounds, and two more survived despite being shot, but we fought them off.

"The days continued peaceful, much to our relief, and hot. That is until one night in early September, just as we neared the Licking River, our lookouts heard canoes approaching from both sides of the river. A storm approached from the west, but fire arrows lit the night sky as well as lightening. We fired back with our rifles and muskets at the shapes we could see when lightening lit the sky. One of the flatboats caught fire; horses and men screamed. Some men jumped aboard from another flatboat to help put out the fire. I feared all would be lost. I worried about my wife and children.

"Yet within minutes a severe storm overtook our boats. The wind and river tossed us hither and fro, but the rain drenched the fires and prevented more Indians from attacking. By morning, nothing could be seen of the Indians.

"As luck would have it, we had storms on and off for the next few nights. While we would see the Indians during the day, the storms kept them near the shores at night.

"We praised God and thanked him for our survival. Many a story of flatboats burned and families killed had reached our ears at Marietta. But Colonel Hinkston guided us to the Licking River, and we managed many miles down the river on our flatboats due to its being a bit higher because of the severe storms.

"Finally, we left our flat boats and took to the land once again with all of us grateful for being back on God's earth. Sarah, the children, and I led our livestock, but I had the foresight to pack two wagon wheels and an axil on our boat. Using lumber from the boat's sides, I created the cart, so we could carry most of our belongings south to this cabin."

I had listened in awe to Edmund's story and realized how difficult their journey must have been. Can you imagine traveling for days on a hot, dirty boat in the middle of a river, with the danger of Indian attack lurking just around every bend? I asked Edmund a few questions about their trip. He answered politely, but seemed curious that I didn't know certain things about wilderness travel.

"Did you build this cabin yourself?" I asked.

"No, one of the men who came in 1775 with Hinkston built it. But he was killed by

Indians while returning with his family. So I registered for his land." he answered, stifling a yawn.

I noticed Samuel lay dozing on a blanket in front of the fire. Sarah had already placed Leah and Abigail on pallets near their parent's bed. Sarah looked tired as she rocked in her chair.

It had been a long day, so I excused myself. Samuel and I climbed the ladder to his loft bed. I thought I wasn't sleepy, but soon I felt my eyes close.

9
A Note from Mom

Samuel and I awoke to the sound of his mother beginning to fix breakfast. As we rose, Samuel moved a tiny flap of leather in the eave of the cabin and looked out, carefully checking out the surrounding area. I couldn't figure out what he was doing. We quickly dressed, having not really undressed, and climbed down the ladder. Edmund sat below on the edge of the bed and continued to fasten his moccasins. He yawned several times. Once finished, he and Samuel moved from window to window, rifle slit to rifle slit, again looking carefully around the clearing outside the cabin. Suddenly I knew—they were looking for signs of Indians!

Sarah served a hearty breakfast of corn mush with honey, corn bread with butter and honey, and some leftover stew. Edmund and she drank a rich smelling tea. I noticed neither put milk in their tea, and only the young child Leah drank milk. I figured it was because their only cow was also feeding a calf, so there was not much to spare.

After we ate, Sarah and Abigail began to clean up while Samuel and I did the milking, carried water, and fed the livestock. Since it was Sunday, the family took seriously the day of rest. After a brief reading from the Bible, Samuel and I played checkers on a cool homemade board. Abigail read a book she had borrowed from a friend at the Station, and Leah played with a cloth doll with an embroidered face.

Edmund alternated between napping, whittling, and reading. He mostly sat on a stump that sat outside just to the left of the door. Sarah, however, continued with her daily routine of cooking, except when she took advantage of Edmund being home to take a short nap. The day turned hot, and Samuel and I did a bit of swimming at a spot in the creek. It really wasn't deep enough, but we had fun.

The next morning started just the same. After breakfast, Abigail brought the butter churn to the porch, while Edmund loaded a tote sack with some venison slabs wrapped in cloth, corn pone, and a few hand tools. He and Samuel picked up their firearms as we left the cabin.

It didn't take us long to walk back to where I had met them two days earlier and to take up the work of clearing stumps. Awfully soon, I realized what hard work really is. My palms blistered, my arms and legs ached, and I roasted under the midday sun. Using the mule for pulling strength, we dug around every stump and used a crowbar-type iron lever to help pull each root from the ground. As the stumps broke loose, Samuel led the mule to the edge of the clearing to a large pile of stumps and dead branches. Edmund planned to burn the pile at the end of the summer.

When we found large stones, especially the flat ones, we carried them to the edge of the field where Edmund used each to build a rock wall around the clearing. I had often wondered how all of those rock walls you see on Kentucky backroads were built. Now I knew and had even helped!

We continued to work until late in the afternoon. I have never been so tired in all my life. I ached all over. I don't think I was cut out to be a pioneer. Finally, we walked back to the cabin. Samuel and I did all of the chores again. Sarah served another stew for the evening meal, again with cornbread. I knew, from listening to Mom, that wheat flour and real bread were rare in *Kentuck* during the early years.

After washing up in the creek and telling Leah a bedtime story, my version of Snow White, I just wanted to go to sleep. So I crept up the ladder and collapsed on my pallet. I don't even remember lying down.

Another day passed about the same. We ate, we worked, we watched for Indians, and we slept. I started to get use to the routine; however, I constantly had the feeling I had traveled here for a reason. I also knew I could not go back alone to where I had time traveled. The danger of Indian attack seemed too real to take such a chance with my life.

On the 17th of June, about noon, a voice rang out from a short distance away hailing Edmund by name. He answered back, and awhile later a short, muscular man came into view. Like Edmund, he wore moccasins, carried a rifle, and had his long dark hair tied back in a ponytail with a thin leather strap. Edmund walked over to greet the man, and they began to talk quietly. Several times each glanced in my direction, but I just kept working. Finally, Edmund called me over and introduced me to his neighbor Patrick Mahan. Mr. Mahan asked me several questions about the dead man who had carried the letters and my escape from the Indians. Edmund and he briefly discussed going to find and bury the body, but decided it was too risky. Mr. Mahan planned to move his family to the abandoned blockhouse at Hinkston's Station for a while, just to be safe, due to the increased Indian activity in the area. I later found out he had seven children! Edmund agreed to discuss such plans with Sarah later that day.

At breakfast on the 18th of June, Edmund told us he was headed toward Hinkston's Station to get the news and to help Mr. Mahan with a wagon wheel. He allowed how Samuel and I could work alone for the morning and could go hunting in the afternoon. Samuel asked if we could stay out after sunset if we stayed within a mile of the cabin. Although Sarah spoke out against the plan, Edmund agreed. Taking his rifle, he set out for the Station. Only then did I realize Sarah also had a rifle. She always kept it loaded and propped nearby.

Samuel and I worked fairly hard that morning and got one stump all the way out and another tree cut down using a two-man saw. Sometime just after noon, we hurried back to the cabin and did the evening chores before eating another bowl of stew for lunch. Sarah packed us some cornbread, jerky, and a few ripe wild plums in a woven cloth bag.

About two o'clock, Samuel gathered up his musket, powder horn, hat, a jacket, a long piece of heavy rope, and a large knife. I had my knapsack. That crazy song "a hunting we will go" kept running through my mind. I think I heard it on a Elmer Fudd cartoon.

Anyway, Samuel and I, after working together for two days, now knew each other kind of well. He was usually quiet, but had a great sense of humor. He was smart and knew lots of things about the forest and hunting. He knew how to look for signs of Indians, where the good hiding places were, and all of the places to find ripe berries. It was a bit early in the summer for most berries, but we did find a few ripe blackberries.

We quietly traipsed through the woods to a place Samuel knew the deer came to drink. We lay down behind a large log to rest and watch. Just before dusk, a large doe with a fawn stopped to drink, but Samuel just watched and let her go on to graze. I'm glad he spared the mother, it would have been like Bambi all over again.

About an hour later, a five-point buck crept slowly, reluctantly, from the edge of some dense undergrowth toward the creek. Samuel motioned for me to be quiet and then took careful aim with his musket. The sound of that thing firing just about blew my ears off my head! My head rung with the racket, and I yelped just about as loud and grabbed both sides of my head. I covered my ears and tried to stop the ringing! Samuel laughed so hard he was rolling on the ground. Good thing he got his buck because

I didn't want to suffer that agony again. The ringing in my head continued for hours. Next time I would know to cover my ears and lower my head!

Now, hunting deer with a musket is not like hunting moose with a spear! But here I was again, deep in the woods with a dead animal to transport back to camp. I helped Samuel string up his deer using the heavy rope and cut its throat for the blood to drain out. I was wondering how we would transport it back to the cabin when he volunteered to go after the mule. I remained behind with the dead deer to keep off predators, such as wolves and coyotes. Samuel handed me the musket and helped me reload. I have fired black powder weapons with Dad so I was not a complete novice. I am actually a pretty good shot—if I do say so myself.

After washing up in the creek, I took up sentry duty behind the log while Samuel left for the cabin. After a while I dug in my knapsack for one of the candy bars and enjoyed a little snack. As the sun set, the wind picked up and dark clouds approached. I untied my jacket sleeves from my knapsack to put it on. I then built a quick shelter of cedar branches. There are lots and lots of cedar trees in central Kentucky so I didn't have to wander far to find enough downed branches.

Finally, I settled in to wait. I knew Samuel would be awhile returning. I tried reading, but kept getting distracted. As I turned to place my book back in my knapsack, I noticed the candy wrapper and reached to place it in my jacket pocket. That's when I discovered the pocket already held a piece of paper. It read:

Greg,
I hope you are having fun and keeping safe. I am so glad I warned you about your next time travel adventure starting from Hinkston's Station. I hope you are enjoying 1778. One more thing I didn't want to tell you ahead of time, if you meet someone you know, try NOT to act surprised and blurt out their name. Oh, and you need to be in Boonesborough by 20 June.
Love, Mom

Really, she warned me? NOT! Who was I going to meet? Her? How was I going to get to Boonesborough in two days? Why would I want to? I knew what was going to happen in Boonesborough in 1778.

10
Traveling South

It took another hour, a rather scary, exciting hour, before Samuel returned. Actually, I hoped all of that time he would not return. Right after I read Mom's note, I heard voices. Indian voices. They seemed really close. I burrowed down behind the log, under my shelter of cedar branches, and slowly, ever so slowly pulled it lower down over my head. For the past hour, I had heard thunder in the distance, and now it grew even closer. From deep in my hiding place, I listened carefully to the voices as they moved through the woods. I hoped they would continue on their way, but also away from the Rittenhouse cabin. It occurred to me that Sarah and the girls might be home alone if these Indians attacked.

I tried to breathe deeply to slow my heart rate and keep from screaming. I kept remembering that scalped body on the creek bank. I kind of liked my hair on my head rather than on someone's belt. Time moved ever so slowly, creeping along minute by minute. The thunder increased making it harder to hear them moving about. Then the rain came all at once. A wild downpour of rain, bits of hail, and wind. My shelter did little to keep me dry, but at least it seemed to keep me out of sight. Just in the heaviest part of the storm, the Indians, five of them again, walked out of the woods at the edge of the clearing and spotted our deer.

Despite the rain, in no time at all, they managed to cut it down, hack it into four large pieces, after gutting it, and carry it off. Yes, they left. I lay there not moving for at least half an hour, before I heard Samuel moving toward me from the direction of the cabin. When he reached my hiding place, he called my name in not much more than a whisper. I poked my head out and replied just as quietly.

Before he could say anything, I blurted out, "Samuel, five Indians took our deer."

Seems he already knew as he had been watching from nearby. He had been coming back with the mule when he noticed their tracks. He returned to the cabin where he left the mule, warned his mother, and then slipped back into the woods to come for me. He might not be much of a talker, but Samuel was one brave dude!

We took a short cut back to the cabin through dense growth so we would not leave many obvious tracks. It was just after dark, and although the storm had passed there was little moonlight to guide our way. As we neared the cabin, we both paused to listen and heard his father's voice. He had arrived back home only minutes before. We listened as Sarah interrupted him to tell of Samuel's warning and that we were still out.

The family spent the rest of the evening preparing to go to the Station at first light. Edmund felt it was the safest place for his family.

We packed food stuffs, clothing, and the few valuables the family owned. They would have to leave their furniture and some of their livestock. They would take their cow and calf, mule, and horse to the Station.

I repacked my knapsack as Samuel and I settled down to sleep. We each took turns keeping watch during the night. Edmund took the first watch, then Samuel, and then Sarah. I took the last watch. I found it very hard to go to sleep. No matter how I tried *not* to think about it, I had now *escaped* twice from being captured or killed by Indians.

The next day, the 19th of June, dawned wet and overcast. The sky drizzled rain while we loaded the wagon, fed the livestock, and closed up the cabin. Everything that could be moved inside was moved, except the pigs and chickens. Edmund and Samuel opened the pig pen gate so the pigs could wander to find food and water. Finally, about 8:00 a.m., they hitched the mule to Edmund's small, hand-built wagon, placed Leah on top of their belongings, tied the cow to the back, and drove off toward the Station. Sarah drove, and Edmund rode the horse.

Samuel, Abigail, and I walked. I carried Sarah's rifle since she had both hands busy driving the mule. Abigail made sure the calf kept up as it followed its mother. Edmund sometimes scouted ahead, but mostly he stayed with the wagon and watched the woods. We walked as quietly as possible. No one spoke above a whisper.

About noon we approached where Hinkston's Fork joined Stoner Creek which ran south toward Martin's Station. Edmund intended to go on to Hinkston's Station. I knew I could follow Stoner Creek, south to Stroud's Creek, past Stroud's Station to the Kentucky River and Boonesborough. But could I make it on my own that far? I needed to be in Boonesborough by tomorrow according to Mom's note. I kept wondering why Mom wanted me in Boonesborough. She knew Boonesborough's history.

Just as we arrived at the junction, we heard voices speaking English. Thank goodness, they were not Indians! Edmund and Sarah recognized the voice of Captain John Duncan. As we approached, Edmund called out. An impressive man, Captain Duncan stood about 6'

3" and was powerfully built. His wife, who stood beside him, was a tiny thing, only about 5'3". She carried a small baby in a pouch. Captain Duncan led a horse packed with their goods.

"Howdy, Edmund, Sarah, headed for Hinkston's?" Duncan asked.

"Yep, too many Indians in our area to feel safe. Some five braves took a deer from the boys last night. They were lucky to escape." Edmund replied quietly.

"Yeah, seems we might be in for a spot of trouble, best to be in a station rather than out at your homestead alone. Ruth and I are headed to Stroud's. Her sister's family is there, and her baby is due any day now."

At that point, Captain Duncan noticed me and Edmund introduced us and briefly told my story. I knew this might be my only chance to get to Boonesborough. So I asked, "Might, I travel south with you, Captain Duncan? I'm a bit anxious to get to Boonesborough and see if my father and brother are there."

"Seems like a good plan, son. We'll be happy to have you along. Can you shoot that rifle?" he asked.

"Yes sir, my father taught me. But this is not mine, it's Sarah's," I explained.

"Not to worry, not to worry, son. I have an extra."

So I said goodbye to the Rittenhouses, hugged Sarah and Leah, and turned to leave. I promised to send word if I could not find my family, then turned south with Captain Duncan and Ruth. We walked quietly along a path beside the creek. I now carried the Captain's extra rifle. We didn't stop to eat, but Ruth pulled corn pone and dried meat from a pouch. We drank from the creek when thirsty. The rain continued on and off all day.

I walked about 30 miles that day. My feet blistered, from being wet in ill-fitting leather shoes and wet socks. The rain kept us all wet and miserable, but finally, long after dark, we reached Stroud's Station. The captain and Ruth settled down after a quick bowl of stew in a small cabin with her sister's family. I found a spot on the floor of the blockhouse and with a borrowed blanket collapsed into a deep sleep.

I awoke to the agony of the feet! I could not even stand. One of the many others who had slept in the blockhouse heard my moans and came over to investigate.

"Young man, you have scald foot! How far did you walk? Don't you know no better? Son, you need you some moccasins!" an old man stated as he examined my feet. I checked him out when he wasn't looking. He appeared to be about 90 years old, thin, wiry, long gray hair, and a beard that hung down past his belt.

Soon he had called over an even older woman, at least she looked older, and he called her Granny. She would have been about 150 years old to be his granny! She used warm milk to wash my feet and applied a poultice before wrapping each in clean strips of cloth. She also brought me grits with honey and butter and a glass of milk to drink. I was just beginning to feel human when I remembered I needed to get to Boonesborough that day! I knew walking the rest of the way, about 10 miles, would be impossible.

Finally, I worked up enough courage to ask, "Do you know of anyone traveling to Boonesborough today?"

I then told them my story and why I needed to get there—the made-up story that is. With a bit of grumbling under his breath about "fool boys having to get to Boonesborough" the man limped away to ask about. I could see one of his knees didn't seem to work quite right. He used a stout cane to hobble along. Maybe if I had a cane? Or crutches?

With not much else to do, I limped over to a window, more of a rifle slit really, and checked the weather. Clear and sunny. Well at least I would be dry.

Determined to make it to Boonesborough, I worked to pull on those now very stiff and still a bit wet leather shoes. Yet, nothing I tried made them go on my feet. They just would not bend enough to get them on over the bandages.

Soon, once again, the stranger came to my rescue. The old man reappeared with a pair of moccasins. They were soft deerskin with no decoration. He fitted them to my feet with great care and showed me how to stuff bits of wool fiber down into the bottom to provide padding. He also instructed me to smear them with bear fat to keep them soft and waterproof. Just where was I going to get bear fat??

Just as I thought all hope of making it to Boonesborough that day was lost, my new friend began to tell me of a wagon headed to the fort.

"I talked a fellow going to the fort into lettin' you ride in his wagon. Sure hope you kin shoot a rifle, cause I 'vinced him you's a crack shot. Don't you go makin' a liar out of me. You better keep 'wake and watch for Injuns," he instructed me.

"Yes, sir, mister? Sorry, I don't know your name," I replied.

"No mister, just Peter, Peter Smith. My wife is Lizzie, she's packin' up some vittles for your journey. Looks like you could use a bit of feedin' up."

So, I gathered my belongings, leaving behind those darn leather shoes, trudged out to the stockade yard, and prepared to move on down the road. Or trail.

Peter introduced me to a quiet man, about 40 years old, who was headed south to Boonesborough. I climbed aboard his small, heavily-loaded wagon, pulled by two rangy mules, and off we went. Back into Indian country. Oh, yeah, all of *Kentuck* was Indian country!

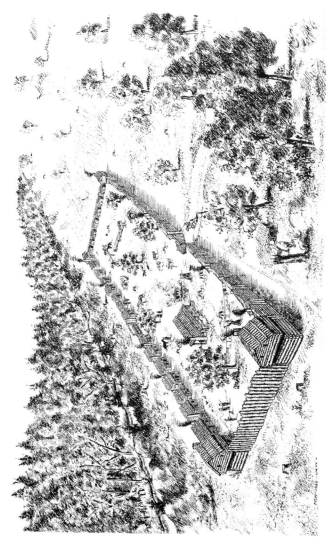

Boonesborough Just Before the Siege

11
Boonesborough

My day proceeded at the pace of a half-dead snail. I sat on a pile of stinky, and I do mean really smelly, animal skins amidst some dead turkeys, cabbages, and other stuff atop a rickety wagon while we traversed a rough trail through forests, meadows, and streams. Just in case you missed that, I DO MEAN ROUGH! I bounced up and then back down all the long day as the wheels rolled over small branches, tree roots, and rocks, large rocks and small rocks that littered what they called a trail.

Occasionally, we passed a small clearing where a log cabin stood. Small cleared fields sprouting crops of corn and other vegetables surrounded most of the cabins. A few men and boys waved as we passed. We didn't see a woman or girl all day. At other cabins, we saw no sign of life. A few even looked deserted. I guess those families had given up and returned east.

While my driver always lifted a hand in reply as we passed other frontier folk, he spoke not a solitary word all day long. Not one word. Didn't ask my name. Didn't ask why I was traveling alone. Didn't say one word. Strange! Right?

Just before noon, I got really bored. I was trying to take my mind off my sore feet and my now sore backside, so, I reached in my knapsack for the Boone book. It wasn't there. I frantically searched my whole knapsack as if I could overlook something as large as a 500-page hardback book! Nope it wasn't there! Then I remembered, I had been reading it when I found Mom's note. I must have left it under the cedar branches when Samuel returned. Darn, Darn, Darn! (I am not allowed to curse.)

Just after midday, we could see the Kentucky River more clearly on our left. My driver—don't know his name as he never talked—clucked to the mules and shook the reins. We began to travel just slightly more quickly. The path now showed more and more evidence of frequent travelers. We also passed more cabins as we approached Boonesborough.

Just as we pulled into the clearing around the fort, a call went up from across the Kentucky River. A man stood on the north shore and shouted for someone to cross and ferry him back to the fort. We could see several men moving cautiously toward the river, while others gathered in small groups to discuss the situation. Some picked up their long rifles and surveyed the surrounding trees. Others seemed angry, others shocked, but even more seemed happy to see the man.

I had just read about this very event in early Kentucky history in the now lost book. That's when I realized I had reached Boonesborough at the exact moment in time that the great Daniel Boone had returned from his captivity by the Shawnee. Wow!

As a couple of the residents rowed a small boat across the Kentucky River, I thought about how Daniel had been gone from *Kentuck* for a little more than six months. I remembered the story in great detail, having just read it.

You see, on 1 January of 1778, Daniel led a party of men north toward the Ohio River to the Lower Blue Salt Licks with a load of iron kettles to boil down the salty water for salt. Pioneers rarely had enough salt as they used it not only for seasoning, but for curing meats, fish, and even hides. Given the great demand, Boonesborough's residents seemed to always be desperately low.

Once they reached the Licks, the thirty men worked day and night that cold, snowy winter to chop wood and keep the fires burning under the salt kettles. Daniel kept the company in fresh meat by ranging far and wide hunting for deer, bear (bear meat was a favorite), and turkey. He also kept a sharp eye for Indian activity. Every few days, some of the men would go back to the fort with the salt packed on horses and return with additional supplies for those at the camp.

The Lower Blue Licks spring supplied thousands of gallons of salty water each day. The men needed to boil about 550 gallons to make 50 pounds of salt. With hard work, day and night, the men made about 500 pounds of wet salt each day. After working all through January, the first crew returned to the fort. Others came out to work.

On the 7th of February, Boone hunted some distance from his brand new son-in-law Flanders Callaway and his friend Thomas Brooks. Flanders and Thomas hunted different areas to bring enough meat into the camp. About midday, Daniel killed a bison (yes, bison used to live in Kentucky), packed the meat on his horse, and headed back to camp in a blinding snowstorm.

Things then went all wrong. Truly, scary, wrong! Daniel noticed four young Shawnee warriors approaching. He tried to drop the meat from his horse to escape, but discovered his knife was frozen in its sheath. He had forgotten to wipe the bison blood from the knife! So, he deserted his horse and took off running. Now Daniel was still a very fit man, but he could not outrun the much younger warriors. One young warrior managed to cut loose the bison meat and mount Boone's horse. Knowing he could not outrun a horse, Daniel leaned his rifle against a tree and surrendered.

He soon learned from his excited captors how Shawnee Chief Blackfish was camped nearby with more than 100 warriors. They had marched south, in the dead of winter, to attack the fort!

As Boone arrived at Blackfish's nearby camp, the warriors greeted him like an old friend, shaking hands and slapping him on the back. The capture of the great white hunter Daniel Boone created excitement among the Shawnee who knew of Daniel's exploits and considerable hunting skills.

All the time since his capture, Daniel kept thinking about Boonesborough, which stood only about a day's journey south by horseback. He knew its stockade walls stood incomplete. Daniel also knew the fort held only a few men along with the women and children and older folks. Thinking hard of a way to save the fort, he decided to lead the Shawnee to the salt party instead!

So, Daniel guaranteed Chief Blackfish the men would not resist being captured if Blackfish promised not to torture them or force them to run the gauntlet. He also told Blackfish he would be happy to come live with the Shawnee. He said in the spring he would help Blackfish capture the fort's women and children so they could all live together like brothers and sisters.

The next morning, Daniel led his captors back to the salt lick where the boilers were enjoying a day of rest. The men watched as Daniel approached, expecting him to bring in fresh meat. Then they spotted the Indians! As they reached for their rifles, Daniel shouted, "Don't fire—if you do, all will be massacred!"

The Shawnee took captive all twenty-seven men, including Daniel. Flanders Callaway and Thomas Brooks had not returned to camp, and one man was away with the packhorses.

Many of the younger Shawnee still wanted to kill the prisoners and attack the fort. They tried to convince Chief Blackfish to go ahead with their original plan. But good ol' Daniel made a speech using a translator and his eloquent words began to sway the chiefs. So, Blackfish called for a vote. Sixty-one warriors voted to uphold the deal they had made with Daniel. The other fifty-nine voted to kill the prisoners and attack the fort. Daniel's plan had worked.

The prisoners knew their problems were not over. The Indians began marching them toward the Ohio River. As they camped the first night near the Licking River, the Shawnee forced Daniel to run the gauntlet. Seems he had been promised only that his men would not have to endure this torture. As Daniel prepared himself to run between the two rows of warriors, he knew many men had died while running the gauntlet. Each warrior would try to attack the runner with tomahawks and clubs. If the gauntlet took place in a village, after the rows of warriors would come the squaws who were just as cruel with their blows.

Daniel had a plan as he started his run between the rows of Indians. He ran fast and then slow. He zigzagged, he dodged, he sidestepped, and even shouldered several warriors aside, pushing them into others along the lines. As he neared the end, one warrior stepped into his path, ready to deliver a deadly blow. Daniel instead lowered his head and butted the man in the stomach so hard he flew backward into the cold, wet snow. As Daniel reached the safety post at the gauntlet's far end, the Shawnee laughed and pointed at their fallen brother. Daniel stood next to the post covered in his own blood, large lumps forming on his head, and with several severe cuts and many bruises, but he had survived.

For days, the Shawnee forced the men to march northward. Their ultimate destination was the British fort at Detroit (now in Michigan) where they planned to sell them to the British for 100 pounds sterling each. The weather remained bitterly cold. They marched along with little food, crossing many icy rivers and streams.

When they reached the Indian town of Chillicothe (in what is now Ohio), the Shawnee held a great war dance. Then, ignoring their agreement with Daniel, they forced the prisoners to run the gauntlet. Many of the salt boilers ended the gauntlet with severe injuries.

The Shawnee adopted Daniel and sixteen of the salt boilers. Blackfish himself adopted Daniel and gave him the name Shel-tow-ee which means Big Turtle. The Shawnee took the other ten men onto Detroit and sold them. Daniel alone of the adopted men made this trip north with Blackfish. He met the British Governor Hamilton who had, of course, heard of the legendary Daniel Boone. Hamilton even offered to help Daniel if he would persuade the citizens of *Kentuck* to side with the British. You see, most frontiersmen sided with the patriots against the British during the American Revolutionary War. Instead Daniel just showed Hamilton his commission as a captain in the Virginia militia and returned south with Blackfish. Daniel was very proud of his appointment as captain and carried his commission wherever he went for the rest of his life.

When they got back to Chillicothe, Daniel discovered one of the salt boilers, Andrew Johnson, had escaped. All the time he was a prisoner, Johnson had pretended to so be feeble-minded the Shawnee were convinced he would get lost and die before getting back to Boonesborough. Daniel knew Johnson actually had great skill as a woodsman and was just pretending. Johnson, of course, made it to the fort at Harrod's Town and with a group of men raided Indian towns north of the Ohio to recapture horses stolen from the settlements. He also told everyone at Harrod's Town how Daniel was happy with the Indians. Called him a traitor and an Indian lover! The word spread to all the settlements about Daniel being a traitor. Some believed. Others didn't.

I sat on the wagon remembering this story as this legendary man was rowed quickly across the river. I couldn't wait to hear how he had escaped. I wanted to hear his words, see his expressions, and meet Big Turtle.

Besides, I hadn't finished the book. I lost it. I now had to live history to find out what happened. I knew some things about the next few weeks that scared the crap out of me. Why did Mom want me here? What was her plan? Didn't she love me?

Boone's Fight With Two Indians

12
Boone's Story

Boonesborough's residents gathered around Daniel as the canoe reached the shore. Daniel stepped out of the canoe looking more Shawnee than frontiersman. His hair was gone except for a long top knot in back and a closely cropped Mohawk toward the front. There seemed to be a bit of stubble where the hair began to grow back on the sides of his head and his face.

He wore a leather breechclout and moccasins. Of course, most of the frontiersmen wore moccasins, even me! He had a hide shirt trimmed in little red and blue trade beads. He carried a rifle with a weird-looking stock and little else. He did have an Indian knapsack and his hunting knife.

Some residents greeted Daniel with anger and shouted out he was a black-hearted traitor. Others seemed relieved to have their leader back. Many more stood silently aside and waited to hear his story. I hopped off the wagon and tried to get close so I could hear his words. The book had described him as a brilliant orator, a person who could make people believe anything he told them. I figured I was about to find out.

Daniel raised his voice to be heard above the crowd. Then he began shaking hands and greeting those he knew. He stopped and took the time to introduce himself to the newcomers, those who had arrived during his captivity. Some men refused to shake his hand and waited for his explanation of events. He greeted Flanders Callaway, his son-in law, with a hug, and asked about Jemima, his daughter. He looked around the crowd as if searching for someone. That's when Flanders told him his wife Rebecca had taken the children and gone east to be with her family. She believed, like many others, he was dead.

Daniel finally began to speak to the crowd saying, "Yep, I lived with the Shawnee. Yep, I told them I would help to capture this fort. I lied. I did all I could to survive. I learned and listened. I made plans. I listened and learned as Blackfish drew maps in the dirt showing the various Indian towns, memorizing those dirt maps. From the beginning, I hoarded powder and shot for the day I would make my escape. Yeah, ol' Chief Blackfish called me *son*, but he never trusted me. I always had a shadow when I rode out of the village to go a huntin'. Those Shawnee gave me just enough powder and shot for one or two loads. But, I fooled 'em. I used half charges almost every time! I kept the rest hidden in a secret pocket sewn inside my shirt.

"Now you see, they learned I knew a bit about gun smithing, so I had to repair their rifles. While repairing a bunch of broken rifles and muskets, I hid away this barrel and lock," he said holding up his rifle for all to see.

"All this time, Blackfish recruited more and more warriors for an attack on Boonesborough.

I told my fellow captives I would help them escape with me. Sadly, the opportunity never came. Then my Indian father allowed me to go with his men to Salt Creek to make salt. Many days later, when we left the salt boiling, I had my chance to escape. The warriors and Blackfish rode off to kill some turkeys they had spotted, leaving me with the squaws. Now, my horse was loaded down with the kettles, but when I saw my chance, I cut the load from my horse. I stopped just long enough to tell my Indian mother I wanted to visit my squaw and children and then I rode off. I could hear her begging me not to go.

"I rode hard, so hard my horse collapsed from under me. I removed my saddle and hung it on a tree. 'magine it's there still today, 'nless someone done found it! So I took to running in streams where I could to hide my tracks. Figured ol' Blackfish and the rest of the Shawnee were right behind me. Probably heard those squaws a wailing when I rode off!

"Well now, it took a bit, but I finally reached the Ohio. Lashed me together a downed log with grapevines and used it as a raft for my rifle and powder. Now, swimmin' that river is a bit of feat. Took me miles downstream it did 'fore I could reach the southern shore. Exhausted, cold, and wet, but with dry powder, I walked 'til twas just too dark to see. Just put myself on the ground and took a little nap.

"Woke up to blistered feet just as dawn approached. Used a bit of oak bark to soothe my aches and soon took to walkin'. Found a bit of sourwood and whittled this stock as I walked. Made it as far as Blue Licks yesterday. Being down right hungry, I shot a bison and enjoyed me some hump meat. Best food I'd had in days. Come to think on it, the only food I'd had in days!

"Came all this way to tell you Blackfish and those Shawnee are coming for us. Plan to attack us and every home along the way," he finished. Some asked questions but he stood his ground, answered each, and looked every man and woman in the eye.

I knew about the coming attack. I *had* read other things about Boonesborough. I knew Daniel had escaped and traveled about 160 miles, mostly on foot in four days with only one good meal.

The folks began to disperse. Some stopped and talked more with Daniel. Others just walked away muttering. Some stayed outright angry, not believing much he said.

Finally, Daniel walked to the fort, entered the gates, and stood staring. He walked slowly to the cabin he had once shared with Rebecca and his children and went inside. I saw a young woman run toward him calling "Papa, Papa." I figured it was Jemima, his only child left in *Kentuck*.

Carrying my knapsack, I made my way into the fort, looking around as I did. I guess I gawked. I mean, how often do you get to visit an 18th century log fort! The log stockade formed the back of log cabins around the perimeter. On each corner stood a blockhouse taller than the walls. Some seemed to have never been finished. The finished ones each gave a good view of the surrounding countryside. I noticed many of the cabins had dirt floors and only a few had real doors. The others used a hide for a door covering. In places where there were no cabins along the wall, the vertical logs were rotted and falling over or just gone. The interior yard, especially near the cabins, was littered with kettles, milk pans, butter churns, and livestock, mostly chickens. It reminded me of Minecraft when I accidently *created* so many chickens they were everywhere, even on top of other chickens!

Surrounding the fort stood fields of crops like corn, squash, melons, gourds, hemp, flax, and beans. The corn stood only about knee high. Each field had a fence of woven sticks that stood about three feet high surrounding it. A livestock pen held several milk cows and calves. Another held a few horses. Pigs seemed to run wild, rooting up everything they could. I could see why they needed fences around their crop fields.

Not knowing what to do next, I stopped a woman and told her my story—you know, the made up one about my father and brother. She told me no one new had arrived at the fort in weeks. Since they were imaginary people, I really didn't expect them to be there! Nevertheless, she helped me find a place to sleep in one of the blockhouses. She also told me if I would gather firewood and help with chores she would feed me in exchange.

I expressed my gratitude. What else could I do? Mom had a plan. My plan was to play along and see what happened next.

13
Waiting

Next morning, Daniel called together the citizens of the fort. He again expressed his belief the Shawnee would attack. He pointed out the decrepit state of the fort and all the work that needed to be done. Squire Boone, Daniel's brother, and his family agreed with Daniel and others began to fall in line with his way of thinking. Daniel told them that Indian spies watched the fort constantly and reported back to Blackfish every week.

With Daniel and Squire in the lead, work began. Some men cut timber to finish the walls and the blockhouses. Squire, being a blacksmith, helped make hinges and other iron pieces and parts. Other men started digging another well inside the fort. The women and girls gathered firewood, nuts and berries, and stored crops as they became ripe. Lookouts continued to watch for Indian activity.

Boone sent runners to Harrod's Town and the many outlying stations about the imminent Indian attack. I listened as he sent a runner to Martin's and Hinkston's and hoped the Rittenhouses had sense enough to stay put at the station instead of returning to their cabin.

As for me, well, I worked. I did a bit of everything including help dig the well. Being small of stature, I was able to go down into the well hole and help haul up dirt and rocks as we dug deeper and deeper. It was hard work.

One day, I helped Daniel make gunpowder. He had learned the "recipe" from one of the enslaved Africans at the fort. Everyone at the fort knew Uncle Monk, a great hunter and marksman. Monk could also play the fiddle and entertained on many an evening. He had even brought apple saplings to *Kentuck* and planted a large orchard near the fort.

The Kentuckians knew running low or out of gunpowder meant death on the frontier. So some of the men and boys would make trips to local caves to gather guano (bat droppings) so they could leach the saltpeter out. Being a tedious process taking several days, few people knew how to do it correctly. But Uncle Monk did!

Now I didn't have a lot of free time, but what time I did have, I spent working on my marksmanship. You know, shooting a rifle! Now, Squire had an old long rifle he had repaired. Seems its previous owner had been killed. After a few days of working with him building a new magazine (a safe place to store gunpowder and firearms), Squire approached me holding the rifle.

"Greg, Dan'l tells me you're a fair marksman. How about you work for me a few hours each day in trade for this here rifle? Figure you can put it to good use when those Shawnee arrive," he asked.

"Thanks, Mr. Boone, I'll do that."

From that day forward, I had a home and a place to work. I still slept in the blockhouse, and did chores for Mrs. Bryant, as her husband was mostly away hunting. But Mrs. Squire Boone kept me fed, fixed my clothing when needed, and even cut my hair one evening.

I pumped the bellows for Squire Boone as he did his blacksmithing work. The bellows forced air onto the fire making it burn hotter. I developed some real muscles from hauling dirt from the well and pumping those bellows!

I also became really tanned, working without my shirt most days. My feet and hands became tough with calluses. I started wearing my hair longer. I even learned to do without underwear as mine wore out, having brought only the pair I wore. I was too embarrassed to ask one of the women for more *small clothes* as they called them. So, I went commando!

Jane, Mrs. Boone as I called her, kept busy each day, even Sundays. Most of the time, she carried their youngest son Enoch on her hip in a sling, him being less than a year old. Jemima

Callaway helped with little Enoch when she could. Jemima and Flanders lived just next door to Squire Boone.

Now, Jemima, being not much older than I, took pity on me and helped me learn about the ways of the fort. One evening she even shared the story of her capture along with Flanders' two sisters by the Shawnee a year or so earlier and how they had been rescued by her father and other men at the fort. At other times, she and Flanders teased me about knowing so little about frontier life and farming. Flanders often took me hunting with him. I learned how to load the rifle faster than I ever could before.

I should tell you right now, Jemima was beautiful. She was slender, with long dark hair, blue eyes, and a really nice personality. I think I had a bit of a crush on her. I think Flanders noticed. I'm not sure about Jemima.

As the days passed and no Indians attacked, the fort settled down into a routine. Many people began to think Daniel lied about the coming Indian attack. While settlers up along the Ohio River reported seeing Indians and few had suffered attacks, the last part of summer wore on for us there at the fort. The days grew hotter and more humid as July passed slowly by.

Then on the 17th of July everything changed. William Hancock, one of the adopted salt boilers, arrived at Boonesborough naked and exhausted. As the men carried him into the fort, he told Daniel and the others about the coming attack. Sick, starving, and scared as he was, Hancock kept repeating over and over that Blackfish had more than 400 warriors, along with twelve Frenchmen!

Daniel and Richard Callaway, Flanders' father, immediately wrote and sent letters to Col. Arthur Campbell back in North Carolina asking for militia reinforcements and gunpowder. Their letters explained how they expected a siege in about 12 days and had begun to lay in supplies.

Again we waited. I worried about Mom. How did she explain my absence? Had I really been gone for over a month? About the middle of August, I became desperate to reach home and considered making my way back to the Rittenhouse family and then on to the place along Hinkston's Fork where I had time traveled. I planned to try and find the Boone book. I wanted desperately to find out what would happen next. If I found it, I might find out if a 13-year-old boy died in the siege. But of course, if I found it, I probably wouldn't be at the siege.

About that same time, the end of August, Daniel put forth a plan to "quit waitin' around" and go see what the Shawnee were up to. Despite many who disagreed with his plan, Daniel wanted to take about twenty men north across the Ohio to attack the Indian village at Paint Creek Town. They hoped to capture horses and make enough mischief to let ol' Blackfish know we were planning to fight and not just surrender.

At the last minute, I plucked up enough courage to ask, "Mr. Boone, may I accompany your expedition as far as Hinkston's Station?"

After pondering for a minute, Daniel replied, "Sorry, son, but you need to remain here and see if your father shows up. I know that's not likely after all this time, but don't give up hope. Also, I need you here to help keep watch. Becoming a crack shot, if I do say so myself. You keep watch over Jemima and all the women when they go to the river and tend the crops. If your father and brother don't arrive by mid-October, I'll take you north myself. Or back to Carolina if you wish."

So I stayed. I worked. I worried. I hunted. I kept watch. I worried. I kept watch, especially over Jemima.

September came. We waited. Then on the 6th Boone's party returned. They rode into the fort on lathered horses, exhausted, and full of news. Blackfish and the Shawnee had already crossed the Ohio and were almost to Boonesborough.

I learned from Flanders what had happened on the raid. After Boone's party had crossed the Ohio, they ran into a group of Shawnee warriors on their way to join Blackfish. After a skirmish where several Indians were killed or wounded, Daniel sent Simon Kenton, one of the best frontiersmen ever, onto the Indian village to see what was happening there. Kenton returned quickly with the news that the village was abandoned! Daniel realized Blackfish's war party had already crossed the Ohio, headed south.

The men needed to get back to the fort. So riding hard and wide to avoid the Shawnee, they traveled day and night to reach Boonesborough and sound the alarm.

Some help had arrived from Harrod's Town and Logan's Station, about 15 men, but not a word had been heard of the militia. Weeks of hard work had completed the stockade walls. The women and children had collected food and water, but the new well still had not struck water.

And here I stood, stuck in a fort in 1778, where Indians were about to attack!

14
The Siege,
September 6th & 7th

Now, everyone believed Daniel about the Shawnee being about to attack. We closed up the fort, bringing in what livestock and crops we could. We carried water and firewood. We loaded rifles, old muskets, and made lead balls. Others manned the walls and blockhouses. Boonesborough now had about 60 men to defend her from more than 400 Indians.

That evening, we spotted the Indians on the other side of the Kentucky River. Our spies counted about 444 Shawnee, Chippewa, Wyandotts, Cherokee, and Ottawas led by their best war chiefs, along with twelve Frenchmen and one captured Negro slave, Pompey. The Frenchmen, led by Lt. Antoine DeQuindre, represented the British General Hamilton. Daniel and the other men realized Hamilton had provided the war party with about 40 pack horses of necessary supplies, including shot, powder, and rifles. He also paid the Frenchmen to fight for him.

Daniel, Squire, and Will Smith, who was second in command at the fort, gave orders to each family. Then the small group within the fort stopped to pray and ask God for deliverance. All turned quiet as the evening progressed.

I tried to sleep. But with others on guard duty moving about the blockhouse, it was impossible. Finally, I rolled up my blanket and moved out into the fort's interior intending to sleep there in the open instead. Jemima, who had just checked on Flanders (she couldn't sleep either) invited me to her cabin instead. I curled up on the floor near the door, my rifle at the ready, and finally drifted off. I dreamed about Jemima. (Don't tell Rose.)

Not many hours later, I awoke as Jemima stepped over me to pick up her water bucket. I grabbed my rifle and followed her out the gate as she and the other women walked to a nearby stream. Several men, including Daniel also watched over the women and older girls.

Suddenly Daniel called out, "To the fort, back in the fort! Moses and Isaiah, run for the fort!" He had spotted the Indians approaching through the trees. The women quickly disappeared inside the gate. Daniel walked toward his nephews Moses and Isaiah who had been tending some livestock and hurried them along.

Now a different kind of waiting and watching began. The Indians advanced to the large meadow in front of the fort and began building an arbor for the chiefs to sit under. Others set up camps, cooked food, and watched the fort.

Inside we watched as well. Some of the women moved their families to the inside corners of the blockhouses. Others went about their chores like nothing at all was happening.

Sometime later, Pompey approached the fort with a flag of truce calling out, "Capt'n Dan'l Boone."

When Daniel answered, Pompey explained that Blackfish wanted his son to come out and surrender Boonesborough.

"Chief Blackfish, he got letters from that there Govern' Hamilton guaranteein' safe conduct to Detroit for all you settlers," called Pompey.

Several people heard this and again showed their anger toward Daniel, believing he had sold them out to the British. About that time, a loud voice called out, "Sheltowee! Sheltowee!" as Blackfish shouted for his adopted son.

All this time, Daniel just stood, pondering his reply. Made me a tad bit anxious not knowing what the man was thinking.

Finally, to many settlers' dismay, Daniel agreed to meet with his Shawnee father some 60 feet from the fort. I watched as he left the fort. I began to wonder if they were right. Had he sold out the settlers to the British? Was he a traitor? Was I going to be an Indian captive after all? Would we all be massacred? Scalped? *Why hadn't I read that darn book!?*

Daniel, Blackfish, and several other chiefs settled on blankets and began to talk. Young Shawnee held branches over their chiefs' heads to shade them from the hot summer sun. We couldn't hear their conversation inside the fort. We all stood and watched, afraid of what might come.

Blackfish brought forth a wampum belt and handed it to Daniel saying, "My son, one end of this belt is Detroit and the other end is this place. It is your choice which path we will walk together between the two. The red is the warpath we have come here on. The white is peace the path we can take together back to Detroit. The black shows the death of all inside the fort if your people do not surrender."

"My father, during my absence many new chiefs have come here. I must meet with them before a decision can be made," replied Daniel quietly.

After a bit more talk, young warriors carried up some gifts for Daniel, they smoked a pipe together, and then Daniel walked calmly into the fort. Once inside, others closed the gates.

I gathered in with all the rest to hear what Daniel had to say. First he handed some of the women seven bison tongues, gifts from Blackfish, and then he began to talk.

"Blackfish asked for our surrender. Says we'll be conducted safely to Detroit if we do. If we don't, he says they will massacre all the men and children and keep only the young women as captives to become squaws for their young men. Told him I needed time to ponder his offer and discuss it with the other leaders in the fort."

Richard Callaway, who had always believed Daniel to be a traitor, started in again, rather loudly, with how Daniel had betrayed their men at the salt licks. How he loved living with the Indians! He went on and on. Some among the settlers expressed their agreement.

About half of the men wanted to surrender, the other half wanted to fight. Finally, Daniel called for a vote. I wasn't sure if I was allowed to vote, but I had decided to side with Daniel.

As Daniel called out for those who wanted to surrender to step forward, Mr. Callaway called out, "I'll kill the first man who proposes to surrender."

William Smith held with those who wanted to fight. He proposed that be their decision. All voted to fight, with Daniel being the last saying, "Well, well, I'll die with the rest."

Boone and Smith decided to delay telling Blackfish their decision. Daniel called out to Pompey and arranged another parley later that afternoon.

Again, I watched as Daniel left the fort, dressed in his frontiersman garb. Smith, however, donned his militia uniform and looked really impressive in his red coat, buff britches, and black boots. I watched as Daniel, Will, and the chiefs talked and talked. Occasionally, we could hear part of the conversation. Smith kept telling Blackfish it would be too hard on the women, children, and old folks to go all the way to Detroit.

Blackfish replied, "Governor Hamilton gave us these forty pack horses so your women and old folks don't have to walk."

Daniel again told Blackfish the many leaders in the fort would have to be consulted before they gave their answer.

Finally, they all agreed on some guidelines for each side during the negotiations. The Indians would not come closer than 30 feet to the fort. The settlers would not carry arms outside the fort, and the women would be allowed to go to the springs for water. The Indians could eat the corn left in the fields and kill the cattle and other livestock as needed. Our men knew, without question, the warriors would kill all our animals.

Boone and Smith returned to the fort. Both agreed Blackfish knew they were stalling. They also discussed, with all us men, how we could defend the fort. The attackers had no cannon. They would need to scale the walls and as the blockhouses jutted out over the walls this would prove difficult.

To make it appear like we had more men than we actually did, several of the women dressed as men and walked around inside the walls. Others put men's hats on long poles and placed them just at the level of the wall. Several people made straw dummies and dressed them as men. They even gave the dummies old broken muskets!

The old well in the fort held little water, and the new one had never been completed. So I watched as the women used every available vessel and carried water from the springs back inside the fort. I had never witnessed so much bravery. The warriors called out "fine squaws, fine squaws," over and over again as the women and girls carried water from the springs.

Inside the fort, our best marksmen kept careful watch from the loopholes in the blockhouses for Indian treachery.

15
The Siege,
September 8th

After another mostly sleepless night, I rose and enjoyed a bowl of Mrs. Boone's fine cornmeal mush, sweetened with just a bit honey. I milked Jemima's cow and carried in the milk. I took a turn at watch on the stockade wall, carried and chopped firewood, and even took a minute to help Mrs. Boone churn butter.

Now that's hard work. You have to keep the paddle moving at an even rhythm. It takes a long time to make the cream turn to butter and even longer when it is hot, and that day was hot. I had just decided the cream was turning when I heard Pompey call out to the fort.

"Capt'n Boone, Capt'n Boone, Chief Blackfish remembers your tales of your beautiful squaw and daughter Jemima. Send them out, send all the young women out for him to have a look," he yelled.

I turned quickly and saw Jemima's stricken face. Having once been captured by Indians, she held great fear. She looked very pale and clung to Flanders who had rushed to her side.

"Papa, don't make me go," she pleaded in a whisper.

But after much talk, Daniel convinced her and several other young women to stand just outside the fort's gates to be seen. As the young women stepped outside, the warriors began calling again. Pompey translated that they wanted to see the girls' hair. So each removed their combs and let their long hair fall softly down around their shoulders. The Indians called out even louder. Four hundred men can make a lot of noise.

Jemima and the other women returned safely to the fort. Flanders and I made her a cup of herb tea and recommended she rest a bit. I walked out of the cabin to hear several of the men discussing what would happen next.

The day crept along. I walked the walls. I watched the Indians. Then I saw Pompey strut toward the fort calling out for Capt'n Boone. I knew this time Daniel would have to give our answer.

And he did. Daniel, Smith and several others walked right out and bravely gave Blackfish our decision. We would not surrender. A very disappointed Blackfish insisted on more talk the following day.

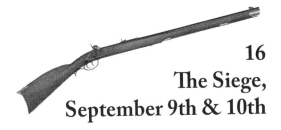

16
The Siege,
September 9th & 10th

The following morning, the women of the fort cooked a wonderful feast of venison and bison tongue, along with fresh corn and other vegetables from their gardens. We men carried out all the tables in the fort to the meadow and set out platter after platter of food for all to enjoy. Indians as well as settlers. Boonesborough's residents wanted to show those chiefs we had plenty of food to withstand a long siege.

I enjoyed the feast, as much as I could while worrying about being scalped! Daniel walked about talking with many of the chiefs. Then after the feast, he and some of the other leaders from the fort met the chiefs at the Divine Elm about 60 feet from the fort. Jemima told me that tree marked the spot, where about three years before, the first Kentucky Convention had been held. I didn't know what that was and without a computer could not even Google it. I remember thinking that when I got home, if I got home, I'd have to look it up.

Anyway, as the rest of us cleared the tables and moved everything back inside, the fort's nine leaders began to talk once more. I had heard Daniel earlier expressing his expectation of a trick. He had placed nine of his best marksmen in loopholes and quietly told them at the first sign of trouble to fire into the group. He told them to aim for Indians, but not to worry about hitting any settlers. He finished with, "Better a few of our leaders being hit than Indians inside the gates."

Standing on the wall, I could see the Indians more clearly than before. As each of our leaders took their seat, an Indian sat on each side of him. Others took a seat or stood just behind. These were not the old chiefs but young, strong warriors. It looked like a trick to me! Several of the warriors and the chiefs, Black Hoof and Black Bird, wore war paint of black and red.

Talking commenced. Daniel, Will Smith, Richard Callaway, Squire Boone, Flanders Callaway, Isaac Crabtree, William Buchanan, Edward Bradley, and John South represented us. All were big stout, strong men. But they were outnumbered, about three to one.

I watched as the talking went on and on. I could see other Indians getting restless. The time passed so, so slowly. Finally, I leaned my rifle against the wall and reached for a drink of water from a nearby bucket. So I missed the first of the action. As I turned back, I could see the warriors and chiefs grab the arms of our men. One of our men broke free and waved his hat frantically. Rifle shots rang out from the fort. Blackfish, who had held Daniel, fell to the ground. Three of our men broke away and sprinted toward the fort.

Daniel, Squire, and Flanders still fought their attackers. One of the warriors swung a great stone pipe and hit Daniel in the back of the head. I was amazed he stayed on his feet. More and more shots rang out. Finally, as all of our men ran for the gate, I raised my rifle and fired at one of the pursuing Indians. I missed.

My whole body shook with fear. I reloaded and tried to calm my breathing. Dad taught me that.

Just before they reached the gate, Squire yelled out and went down. I could see him grab at his shoulder. He had been shot! Flanders ran back and helped Squire into the fort just as the gates swung shut. The heavy log bar fell into place with a clang against the iron rests Squire had fashioned at his forge.

The firing continued, and I saw one elaborately dressed chief fall dead. Then shots rang out from the high cliff on the other side of the river, picking off one of our men lying atop a blockhouse. He tumbled down inside the blockhouse through the opening in the roof. Several men ran toward him expecting to find him dead. Nope, he was alive with 14 bullet holes in his clothes and not a scratch on his body. Weird, huh? Or just plain lucky?

Inside the fort, terror raged. Livestock and horses ran frantically stirring up enough dust so that no one could see. Many of the women and children ran to hide in a cabin in the center of the compound. Children cried and screamed. Women cried and tried to sooth their babies. Dogs barked and ran. Even the chickens put up a ruckus, clucking, squawking, and flying in all directions at once.

Again, I tried to calm my breathing. It helped some, but being calmer didn't stop the Indians from advancing. Hundreds of them at a time. Seemed like millions! I reloaded and fired, reloaded and fired, reloaded and fired, again and again. The Indians rushed the walls, hooping and a hollering their shrill war cries. But, Boonesborough's men, and even a few women, stopped them from gaining access to the walls. Many an Indian fell. Each time other warriors would carry off their fallen comrades. It seemed to go on and on and on.

As the day progressed, Daniel kept up a steady stream of encouragement. Passing by each position to help out and fire off a few shots when needed. Random shots killed some of the livestock and women bravely pulled each dead beast aside to a safe spot and butchered it for meat. Other women brought us water along with ammunition so we would not have to leave our posts. We were all now covered with soot, streaks of black powder, and just plain dirt. I guess it was our version of war paint.

A few of the older boys and girls brought us food as the day wore on. I didn't feel much hunger, a lot of thirst though.

Toward the end of the day, I took an outhouse break, then wandered over to Jemima's cabin. She walked up just as I reached the door, and I turned to help her with a pan of milk. Right as I reached for the pan, Jemima yelled out. She grabbed at her backside, you know her butt, and then did the most remarkable thing. She dropped her skirt to her feet, hiked up her petticoat and started grabbing at her backside again. I noticed right off that women's drawers (some people call them pantaloons) had no seat in them. They were just open. I guess so they could use the outhouse without having to strip half naked. I just stood there holding the pan of milk, which was slowly running over the side and onto the dirt, and stared!

Flanders and several of the women ran up about that time as Jemima was still making quite a ruckus. She just kept screaming and searching her petticoat and drawers. That's when the rifle ball fell to the ground. Flanders reached down and picked it up and then dragged Jemima inside the cabin and shut the door. Left me standing there, stunned, holding a half empty pan of milk. I had just seen Jemima Boone Callaway's butt!

Finally, Flanders came back out, and explained. The spent bullet didn't even make a hole in her linen petticoat and drawers, but left a bruise on her backside. Flanders teased her about it for days. How embarrassing to be shot in the butt! I was sure glad she wasn't hurt. She had a nice butt.

Just at dusk, the Indians suddenly stopped rushing the fort, and all fell quiet. So, I slipped down from my position on the wall to go check on Squire. I found Daniel leaving Squire's cabin just as I arrived.

"Mr. Boone, could you tell me please, how is your brother?" I asked.

"Well, son, he's sleeping. Just removed the musket ball from his shoulder. Step in and see Jane, she's worried 'bout you. Says she hasn't laid eyes on you all day. Then go see Jemima for somethin' to eat. I'll be there eventually. Want to check on a few of the men," he replied and walked quietly into the night. He looked tired and worried, like a man who carried the weight of the world on his shoulders.

The next morning dawned clear and hot. They came at us on and off all day. I manned my post the best I could. About noon, Flanders came by.

"Hey, Flanders, how did you men manage to escape with only one man hurt?"

"Well, Greg, you see, one Indian is the equal of four regular soldiers. But us Kentuckians, well, each of us is a match for two Indians. Besides that, well, it was a miracle." And he walked on, smiling.

Oh! Of course, that explained it.

Throughout the day, lead balls thudded into the walls of the fort, the smell of gunpowder hung heavy in the air, and we watched. In the afternoon, the Indians began spreading piles of flax left outside the fort alongside several livestock fences that ran toward the walls. That night they set them on fire. A few of the men, left the fort and amidst a hail of bullets pulled the burning flax and fences away from the stockade walls.

One of these brave men kept yelling obscene taunts at the Indians. Being a well-known curser, John Holder knew quite a few inventive phrases to heap abuse upon our attackers. Once they returned inside, I heard his mother-in-law Mrs. Callaway chastising him for his raunchy language.

"Young man, it would be more becoming to pray than to swear," she stated.

As he walked away, John replied tersely, "I've no time for praying, @#&&*%%$^." (Remember, I'm not allowed to curse, so I can't tell you what word he used.)

17
The Siege,
September 11th to 16th

The morning of the 11th dawned quietly. Bits and pieces of the day before ran constantly through my head. I had slept on the wall, on and off all night. I hurt and was damp with a heavy, morning dew. I replayed the attempted fire and the almost constant assaults of the day before in my head. I also wondered why I was here? Why had Mom insisted I come to Boonesborough? But worrying and wondering didn't give me answers. Nope, none at all, nada!

A while later, during the quiet of early dawn, I heard one of the men call out for Cap'n Boone. Daniel, Flanders, Will Smith, and several other men rushed to the river side of the wall and cautiously looked over into the river. I watched as they kept checking and discussing. Discussing and checking. Next Daniel called out to several men who began gathering up some of the extra logs and wood stashed here and there inside the fort.

Finally, too curious to wait, and I had to well, you know, take care of nature's call, I headed down from my post, used the outhouse, and ran over to Jemima's. Everyone now ran in the stockade yard making it harder for the Indian snipers on the opposite bank.

Flanders filled me in on the morning's discovery. "Couple of men noticed the river being muddy downstream but not upstream. Seems the Indians are tunneling up from the river to under our walls. Probably plan to blow an opening and then rush us. Some of the men are going to build a platform out over the wall so they can make sure. Too risky to go out."

"Oh."

"Others are going to begin digging a trench across where theirs would enter. That way, we can pick them off one by one. I'll call you when your turn to dig comes 'round," he replied and walked away, back to his post.

So we dug. They dug. We built a platform, we kept watch, and we fired a few volleys as they bluffed attacks during the day. The firing didn't stop at night. Actually got a bit heavier, as we fired at their muzzle flashes, and they replied in the same manner.

I learned to fire and then move quickly away from the top of the wall or loophole. I learned this the hard way, as once just after I fired, a returning volley sent splinters of wood into my hat and shirt. Picked them out for the rest of the day. Those sharp little sticks of wood hurt.

When it was pitch dark, little moonlight that night, London, one of the enslaved Africans, crept out of the fort to get off a few shots at the tunnelers. Unfortunately, his rifle misfired. Some lucky warrior aimed at the snap his hammer made and killed London. I didn't know him well, but he had seemed nice enough.

I had struggled since I arrived at the fort with the idea of slavery, having learned many of the settlers brought one or two slaves with them into the wilderness. Most treated them kindly and like family, yet, here they were forced to fight for their lives. Other owners made them work too hard and gave them little food. I kept thinking how these enslaved men and women were fighting for their lives because of someone else. Someone who had forced them to come into the wilderness. Didn't seem fair.

Now London was dead. He wasn't the only one we lost that night. David Bundrin took a bullet to the brain. He didn't die right out. Just sat there with his brains leaking out, rocking back and forth, not saying a word. He passed just before daybreak. His wife kept saying how lucky he was the ball didn't hit him in the eye. I guess grief makes you crazy sometimes.

It was this night that the Indians began using another tactic for the first time. Using arrows with a bit of gunpowder and some punk (crumbly, dry wood) in a bit of cloth, they created fire arrows. One cabin caught and blazed quickly, the only one with a shingled roof. I soon discovered it was hard to throw water high enough to put out the fire. Yet, it was just as dangerous to go up on the roof, because then you could be seen and shot!

Other Indians ran up to the walls and threw lit torches over. Of course, that made them easy targets for our sharpshooters. Most of the torches fell harmlessly into the enclosure. We quickly extinguished with Squire's squirt guns any cabins that caught fire.

I think ol' Squire Boone might have been the first person to make a real water gun. Created out of spare rifle barrels and bags of water, the guns could shoot water several feet upon the roofs. They did help put out the fires. It would have been fun, if not for the Indians on the opposite river cliff shooting at us!

Squire and I had also created a cannon of sorts. We hollowed out a gum tree log with this long auger we heated up red hot and then made iron bands to wrap around it. Squire and I figured it only had one good use, but Daniel kept insisting we would blow ourselves up if we tried to use it.

When things got real tense one afternoon, a bunch of the men loaded up the cannon with powder and buckshot, opened the gate, and fired it at the Indians. However, the cannon proved to be a bit of a bust hitting only a few Indians. I don't think it killed any! Squire came bursting out of his cabin right as they tried it again. Just like Daniel predicted, it blew up into a million little splinters. A few men had to pick splinters out of their hide, but none were seriously hurt.

After that, the Indians had another way to taunt us. Pompey would call out "Why don't you fire your big wooden gun again?" Then the warriors would hoop and holler and laugh.

As the days passed, we threw stones down on the Indians as they tunneled. Now, this seemed to make them really angry, and they yelled back for us "to come out and fight and not try to kill with stones like children." One of the women in the fort chastised us for throwing stones as "it might hurt the Indians and make them mad." I think she missed the point of us throwing rocks! I mean we were also SHOOTING THEM WITH REAL RIFLES! So we threw more stones and yelled, "Don't throw stones, don't throw stones." I doubt we seriously hurt any Indians, but it kept them busy dodging our rocks.

We dug our well. We dug our tunnel. We put out fires. We kept watch. We shot Indians.

Pompey kept taunting the fort and playing a game of chicken with our sharpshooters. He would pop his head up in one place and then another along the trench they used to reach their tunnel. Several men tried over and over again to shoot him. Finally one day, his head popped up, a rifle fired, and no more Pompey. William Collins insisted he was the one to fire the fatal shot, but so did William Hancock. Guess we'll never know.

Now our men taunted the Indians with "Where's Pompey?" The answer always came back that he was sleeping or hog hunting. Several days passed before they admitted he was dead.

Another Indian kept mooning the fort from a tall tree. Just slightly out of rifle range, he would climb to a certain branch in a certain tree, turn around, bare his backside, pat it, and call "Kiss my %&&." After several days of enduring his taunts, Daniel loaded his rifle with an extra load, rested the barrel on a loophole, tested the wind a few times, made adjustments, and fired. The man fell from the tree. Later that day, several warriors managed to carry his body off the field of battle.

Now I don't tell you all this because I think all that death was cool. I was scared, a bit sick to my stomach most of the time, and worried to death. This little log fort held my friends. Real danger threatened their lives every minute of the siege. Also I kept thinking about how I had likely killed at least one man. He probably had a family. Would a wife mourn him when she heard of his death? Would his children grow up without a father? I had a friend from school who lost his father in Iraq. How was his death any worse than that of the warrior I shot? Yet, if I didn't defend myself and my friends here at Boonesborough, we would all perish.

I think learning history first hand, live and in person, might be a bit more than I had wished for. I kept rethinking this time travel business. Why hadn't I asked Mom more about how it was done? But I couldn't leave now, these people needed me!

Day after day, we continued to fight. I learned to sleep through all the racket. I learned to eat when I wasn't hungry. I learned how to reload faster and faster. I learned how to save my ammunition for when it was truly needed. I learned to depend on others. I learned to survive.

Daniel seemed to be everywhere at the same time. He stayed busy making sure everyone else remained prepared. However, one afternoon as he ran across the yard, a sniper's ball caught him in the shoulder. Jemima unwound his neck stock and blood gushed out. After she calmed, we could all see it was just a flesh wound. The women dressed the wound, and Daniel rested for a bit.

As the Indians noticed his absence, they began to chant, "We killed Boone! We killed Boone!"

Awakened by all the racket, good ol' Daniel climbed one of the parapets and shouted back, "No you didn't. I'm here and ready for you!" That shut them up for a while. Of course, he had to duck fairly quickly as they all took aim at him again.

The days now passed all in a blur, but it seems I can remember every minute. We began to run low on water. We gave the livestock as little as possible. We had no food for them so some looked pretty darn thin. We conserved rifle balls and even melted down some of the women's pewter plates to make balls. We picked up stray balls in the stockade and melted them to make new balls.

The fort began to stink from livestock waste, human waste, unwashed bodies, babies' diapers, rotting produce, and dead animals.

Women cooked when they could, but seldom was it enough. We had very little medicine. Children and babies cried. Yet, when the daily attacks began, everyone performed their duties, and we survived over and over.

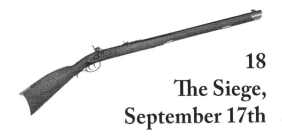

18
The Siege,
September 17th

What can I say, the fighting began nine days ago. Blackfish and his warriors arrived twelve days ago. Yet, it continued. Daniel and Will Smith agreed our attackers are anxious to bring this to an end. We were running low on supplies, not food so much as powder, lead, and especially water.

All day I kept to my post. I searched the hills for the sign of militia coming to our rescue. Late in the afternoon, I fell asleep during a lull in the fighting. I awoke sometime later to Daniel and Will passing by each post, making sure each man had plenty of shot and powder. I could tell they expected an imminent attack.

It came just at dusk. I think every Indian ran or rode his horse toward our walls. They hid fire arrows and torches under blankets and wet hides removing them just as they reached the walls. Now smoke hung heavy inside and outside as several of the cabins caught fire. The acrid smell of gunpowder, the yelling of Indians, the cries of our men from one to another filled the air. Women, children, and babies added their voices to the confusion of sound.

I fired over and over again. One of the women came up, sat beside me and reloaded for me. She had a rifle as well, but I did all the shooting. It seemed to go on and on and on. The night sky, lit as it was with powder, gave off so much light you could read by it. I seemed like a foggy day, except for the noise and the smell.

Despite our best efforts and some very excellent sharpshooting, the fires burned more intensely. Some men climbed on roofs to smother fires with hides and blankets, all despite the continuing sniper fire from the opposite river bank.

We could tell their tunnel now approached our lower wall. A few of our men stayed ready for them to break through, planning to shoot them as they did. Things looked really desperate. Sure wish I had finished that book and knew what was going to happen.

Then it began to rain, at first softly, just a few drops. Then it increased to become steady. Then a bit harder as the fires sputtered, put out even more smoke, and finally died. As the rain became even heavier, their tunnel collapsed!

The rifle fire continued, but not as steady as before. We kept watch all night, expecting them to come at us again. They never came.

As quiet as a mouse, dawn arrived. The clearing in front of the fort seemed deserted. We occasionally heard shots in the distance, but with each passing hour they seemed further and further away. Daniel and several of the men crept out and surveyed the surrounding forest.

The Indians appeared to be gone. They left behind no dead and no wounded. Our women went for water, while some of the men collected cabbages left in the fields to feed the livestock.

I survived. We won. I'd lived through one of the greatest events in America's history. And I still didn't know why I was here!

Later in the day, Daniel and our men reappeared with the news that it was truly over. We had lost only two men and had two or three injured.

I slept like a log that night in mid-September 1778, on the floor of a blockhouse in a stockade in frontier Kentucky, perfectly comfy in a borrowed blanket. I awoke and had just settled in with a bowl of corn mush and some leftover stew when a tall, blond man, dressed in leather and wool, wearing beaded moccasins, and carrying a Kentucky long rifle rode in through the open gates of Boonesborough.

I knew this man ... Dad!

I ran out, not saying one single solitary word, and leapt in his arms. "I'm mighty glad to see you," I whispered.

Some of the women had tears in their eyes watching us. I guess others wondered where my "imaginary" brother was. I didn't care. They didn't ask.

Dad and I talked and ate. I talked, he talked, and I talked some more. I listened as he talked. Seems he had arrived two days before and watched the siege from one of the surrounding hills, him and a man named, William Patton. Patton had been out on a long hunt and arrived two days earlier than Dad. All they could do was hide and watch. After watching the events of the night before, Patton had ridden hard for Logan's Station to tell them Boonesborough had fallen.

Dad had stayed put and made sure all was safe before he rode in. Seeing as how he knew how the siege ended, he kept saying he had not been the least worried about me. Nevertheless, he kept hugging me.

I just kept talking and talking and talking, telling him everything I had experienced. Then

I remembered something, something that had been bothering me for days.

"Dad, I need to go back to the Rittenhouse's cabin and warn them about what will happen in 1780," I whispered.

"No can do, Greg, we have to leave. We have somewhere to be. Your mom and Rose are waiting for us."

"Dad, two questions, well maybe three. First, why is Rose with Mom?"

"You'll find out when we see them, too hard to explain now," he replied quietly.

"Okay, why did Mom send me here?"

"Greg, as a time traveler you have to learn how to survive in various situations. Worked out well for you! You are now a Revolutionary War veteran! If Boonesborough had fallen, the settlements west of the Alleghenies would have had no choice but to side with the British for protection from the Indians. Your victory here makes all of you folks heros of the Patriot Cause.

I think it was destiny or just plain history that I got held up in another time and was not here to meet you in June. Now one more question, then we get moving, okay?"

"But, Dad, don't we have to go back to the spot on the stream where I first time traveled in order to go home?"

Dad just stared at me. "Greg, you could go home anytime you wanted. You are a time traveler, it's in your genes, your DNA. All you need is something from that time, an artifact from the past or your time and the desire to go," he explained.

"Really? But, Dad, what do I have that can take me home?"

"Well, your clothes—we'll discuss those moccasins later—your knapsack, the stuff in it. Any of those things will do."

"So if I take something from this time with me, like this rifle, I can come back?" I asked.

"Sure thing, that's the way it works," he whispered back. "Just let me go speak with my old friend Squire, and we'll be on our way.

"Wait, wait! Dad? You know Squire Boone?" I whispered.

"Of course, who do you think gave him the idea for the water guns?"

Captain Daniel Boone

Historic Facts & Fiction

Boonesborough is no longer a town. Now a Kentucky State Park, the site features a reconstructed fort near the site of the original one.

The *Siege of Boonesborough* took place just as described. All of the names are real and events that Greg witnessed occurred during the siege. Greg and his father are the only fictional characters.

Cumberland Gap was first known as *Cave Gap*. There is a large cave in the Gap that is now closed to the public.

Harrod's Town, or *Fort Harrod* was established in 1774 by James Harrod and several other men. Later renamed Harrodsburg, it was the first incorporated town west of the Appalachian Mountains.

Hinkston's Creek and *Hinkston's Station* were named for Colonel John Hinkston (also spelled Hinkson). Hinkston established his station in 1775. Simon Kenton and Thomas Williams helped build a blockhouse there in 1776. Most of the cabins were abandoned in 1778 but it was re-established as a station in 1779 and renamed Ruddell's Station.

Kentuck or *Kaintuckee* were two of the original names for what is now the Commonwealth of Kentucky.

The *Kentucky Convention*, on 23 May 1775 delegates of the Boonesborough settlement met with leaders of the Transylvania Company at Boonesborough's Divine Elm to draw up laws and a compact between the two parties for the Transylvania Colony.

The site of *Martin's Station* has never been located by archaeologists. A map or plat of its location does exist. Several later stories relate how the Garrard family built a walled cemetery on the same place where the station once stood. Archaeologists have **not** recently carried out excavations to find its location.

The *Rittenhouse* family really lived near Ruddell's and Martin's Stations. At this time, their first names and the number of children is unknown to this author. To learn what happened to the

Rittenhouse family in 1780, Google Ruddell's or Martin's Station.

Stoner Creek is named for Michael Stoner (or Holsteiner). Stoner came to Kentucky with Daniel Boone in the mid-1770s as a surveyor.

Stoner Creek and *Hinkston's Creek* are also called forks and are part of the Kentucky's Licking River water system.

To Learn More

Telling this story would have never been possible with out the research and writings of several Boone biographers. First and foremost the work of Robert Morgan in *Boone: A Biography* provided the facts for Greg's adventure. Morgan's insight into the life of Daniel Boone was invaluable for making the great frontiersman come to life in these pages.

For those who wish to read more, you might enjoy the first Boone biography I ever read, *The Life and Times of Col. Daniel Boone: Hunter, Soldier, and Pioneer* by Edward S. Ellis, published in 1884, or *The Life of Boone* by Cecil B. Hartley.

Easy reading books on Boone include *Who Was Daniel Boone* by Sydelle Kramer; *Daniel Boone: Young Hunter and Tracker* (Childhood of Famous Americans) by Augusta Stevenson; and *Daniel Boone: Frontiersman* (Heroes of History) by Janet Benge. To learn Jemima Boone's story or more about Simon Kenton you can find several books in your local library or stories on the internet.

162

Glossary

archaeological artifact - an object left in the soil by people who lived in the past, such as a pottery sherd, coin, or projectile point

archaeology - the scientific study of how people lived in the past based on artifacts found in the soil

arrow head - the tip of an arrow, called a projectile point by archaeologists

breechclout - a piece of cloth worn around the hips, generally the only item of clothing worn.

British pound sterling - the currency of Great Britain, still used in America during the Revolutionary War.

corn pone - bread made with cornmeal rather than flour, often made without milk or eggs. Either baked or fried, it was hard and dry.

feature - a stain left in the soil by past activities of man, such as a red stain left by a fire. (*Greg's*

163

addition to definition: "As we excavated at what Mom hoped was the remains of Martin's Station, we looked for features. Features are stains left in the soil by the past activities of man. On an historic site, these can be from fires, walls of structures, wells, privies (outhouses, you know toilets), paths and roads, gardens, and even fences. I once found a post hole on one of Mom's historic digs. We figured out what the round stain was when we mapped all the site's features on her computer. As we looked, we noticed this line of round features each about five feet from the previous one. The features formed when the fence posts rotted!")

guano - the excrement of bats (*Greg's definition* - bat poop.)

Kentucky long rifle - the firearm that conquered the frontier and won the American Revolution. Often formed from a flat bar of soft iron, a gunsmith hand forged the barrel before he bored and rifled it with crude tools. He then fitted it with a stock hewn from a nearby tree, like maple or cherry. He hammered a lock to shape on his anvil, as he did all the metal parts and pieces. More accurate than a musket, but slower to load, a rifle was a real treasure, but also a necessity on the frontier.

limestone springs - common in central Kentucky. Springs result when an aquifer (a body of rock that holds water) becomes filled to the point that the water overflows onto the land's surface. Springs range in size from small seeps, which flow only after a lot of rain, to huge, gushing pools flowing with hundreds of millions of gallons daily.

Native American - another name for an American Indian.

neck stock - a long scarf wrapped around the neck and tied, worn by men in the 17th and 18th centuries.

physical anthropologist - a scientist who studies human bones, especially those from archaeological sites.

prehistoric - existing in a period before written history

projectile point - arrow or spear point, usually made of stone.

165

saltpeter - the form of potassium nitrate that occurs naturally, used in the manufacture of fireworks and gunpowder.

screen - a wooden box with a heavy screen mesh bottom used to sift soil to find artifacts.

single pen - one room, a room made from logs is called a pen

spent - as in a bullet that has reached the end of its firing path and is about to fall to the ground.

stone pipe - generally carved from steatite or soapstone, Indians used these for ceremonies, sometimes called peace pipes.

tripod - a stand holding a screen for sifting dirt for artifacts

trowel - a triangular-pointed blade hand tool used by archaeologists

wampum - cylindrical beads made from shells, pierced and strung, used by North American Indians as money, for ornaments, and for ceremonial and sometimes spiritual purposes.

About the Author

C.M. Huddleston is a retired Registered Professional Archaeologist with more than 25 years experience. All of the archaeological terms and techniques described in this book are accurate.

She is also an historic preservation consultant and historian. C.M. lives in rural Crab Orchard, Kentucky, with her husband and their Australian Shepherd Katie.

Learn more about Greg and his coming adventures in time travel at www.cmhuddleston. com.

Teachers, you can find activities and lessons related to both *Adventure in Time* books at www.cmhuddleston.com.

24542926R10100

Made in the USA
San Bernardino, CA
29 September 2015